To Jesse—
When it
storms, dance!

[illegible signature]
Rochester '15

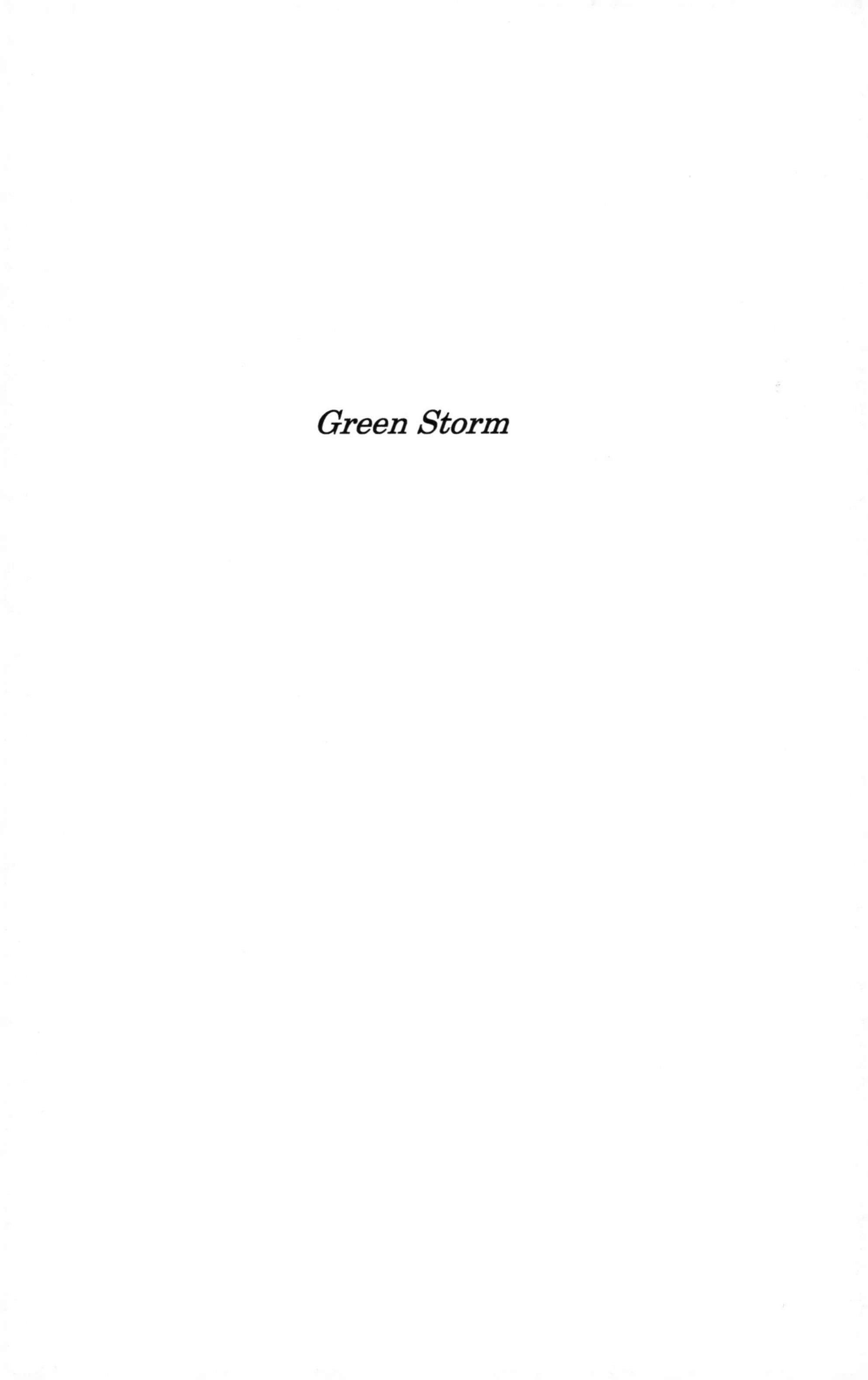

Green Storm

Green Storm

Kaylee O'Shay, Irish Dancer

Rod Vick

Laikituk Creek Publishing

Green Storm

Kaylee O'Shay, Irish Dancer

Laikituk Creek Publishing
Mukwonago, Wisconsin

Manufactured in the United States of America

ISBN: 978-0-6923100-3-8

For all dancers
who have known the pain.

For my mother.

Patience is power;
with time and patience,
the mulberry leaf becomes silk.
- *Chinese Proverb*

One

Riding her bicycle so fast that the wind screamed in her ears, and then rocketing off the ramp in the gravel pit at the end of Stony Hill Road . . .

Scoring the winning goal in a pickup soccer game against the boys who lived along Cranberry Street . . .

Parachuting into the mouth of an active, lava-spewing volcano in order to disarm the terrorist doomsday device hidden in a secret lab at its base . . .

All of these were things that eleven-year-old Kaylee O'Shay would have enjoyed far more than tagging along with her grandmother on the first Saturday morning in September. But Grandma Birdsall had an appointment with Dr. Holland, and Kaylee was the only one without a Saturday morning commitment.

While she loved her grandmother immensely, Kaylee did not exactly love the idea of paging through last year's hunting magazines in a doctor's waiting room on a glorious school-free morning when she could be biking or scoring goals or seeking out an active volcano.

On the other hand, maybe this would not have been the best Saturday morning to jump into a volcano—or even to jump rope, for that matter. She had awakened to it from her "seriously twisted and quite possibly pure-evil" dream, which is what her friend Jackie had called it after hearing Kaylee's description.

Sometimes children dream of falling or of being trapped in dark places. At other times it's monsters—dark and hungry and always just a half-step behind. And more than a few children have been known to dream about arriving at school wearing just their underwear.

Kaylee O'Shay's dreams were the worst of all. They were about soccer.

Not that soccer is a bad thing. In fact, Kaylee often dreamed of heroic successes on the soccer field, dreams that she wished she might return to after she woke. For instance, she occasionally dreamed of March 17th and the season-ending indoor tournament for her Green Storm team. *(Had six months really gone by since that tournament?* Kaylee marveled.) She saw her father, the Green Storm coach, pacing back-and-forth in the team box, urging them on against their rivals, the Kickettes. *(Could such a good team really have such a seriously pathetic and quite possibly pure-stupid name?)* The dream seemed so real—Brittany Hall kicking the game-winning goal, girls screaming and crying in celebration, everyone lifting the championship trophy high into the air.

And her father giving her an enormous hug—just the way it had all happened back on St. Patrick's Day.

But that was not her only soccer dream.

In her other dream—the seriously twisted and quite possibly pure-evil one—it was Kaylee herself who brought the ball upfield, closing on the Kickette goalie. She saw her proud father smiling from the sideline, saw the defenders melt away as she deftly worked herself into position for the shot.

Then the ball would be gone, vanished, as if it had fallen through a hole in the floor at the Paavo Indoor Sports Complex. As she searched frantically for the ball, she would suddenly find herself alone on the artificial turf. Through the glass walls surrounding the pitch, she would see people but would recognize none of them. Worst of all, when she looked to the team box, her father would be gone. She would call out his name, scramble through the box into the outer area of the complex, weave through the sea of unfamiliar faces. Eventually, she would make her way to the parking lot. *Don't leave without me! Don't leave me!* She would dodge cars, out onto the highway, running, running . . .

At this point she would wake up. And the day that followed would usually be horrid.

"I dreamed about soccer again last night," Kaylee reported to her mother as she shuffled to the kitchen table a little before nine.

Her mother offered a sympathetic look, setting a cereal bowl in front of her daughter. "The 'seriously twisted' dream?"

Kaylee, a small green-eyed girl with freckles and dirty-blonde curls, began the ritual of microwave instant oatmeal preparation as she nodded. "And quite possibly pure-evil."

"Most dreams don't mean anything, sweetheart," her mother said kindly as she folded clean t-shirts and underwear on the far end of the table. "They're just random thoughts that we sometimes remember after we're awake."

"But if I have the same dream three or four times, they're not so random anymore," Kaylee argued.

Beth O'Shay, a short woman with wavy-brown hair and almost as many freckles as her daughter, smiled absently as she rolled up a pair of boxers that, based on the outrageous cartoon skateboarder design, must have belonged to Kaylee's ten-year-old, cereal-addicted brother, Will. "You probably miss soccer. That's all it is. I used to have a dream like that when I was a little older than you are."

Kaylee stopped stirring her bowl of oat mush. "What did you miss?"

"Hm?" It seemed to Kaylee that her mother's head had snapped up from the laundry, almost as if she had been awakened from a dream of her own at that moment.

"Your seriously twisted and quite possibly pure-evil dream," said Kaylee. "What was it about?"

Mrs. O'Shay's grip on the boxers appeared to tighten and Kaylee caught a fleeting glimpse of desperation in her eyes. Then, in an instant, it passed, and her mother's smile returned. "After I opened the Stitchin' Kitchen, I sometimes missed teaching. I'd dream I was back in my classroom." Mrs. O'Shay had been an elementary school teacher when Kaylee was younger. Then, almost three years ago, she had decided to follow a longtime dream and open her own business, a combination fabric store and coffee shop. "Usually they were nice dreams, but sometimes the students would disappear and I'd be all alone and I'd hunt all over the school for them."

Kaylee swallowed a spoonful of oatmeal and considered the similarities between her dream and her mother's, both of which seemed to involve people disappearing. "But you weren't my age when you dreamed that. You were old."

Mrs. O'Shay offered a tight-lipped smile. "I just meant that I was younger than I am now." Then she sighed loudly. "I wouldn't worry about it, honey. You've been playing soccer most of your life. It's only natural that you'd dream about it now that you've switched to dancing."

Kaylee saw that this was probably true. The day she had taken her first steps, her father, Tom O'Shay, had rushed out to the store and returned with a miniature soccer ball. "This one's going to be a champion!" he had proclaimed to his wife, watching the tiny girl bump the ball around with her pudgy feet, occasionally tumbling over the top of it. She had begun recreation league soccer at four and had played at least three seasons a year ever since. Tom O'Shay had always been right beside her.

He loved soccer.

"Your father was quite the star in high school and college," Beth O'Shay had told her daughter many times. Tom would generally grumble a rebuttal, something like, "I wasn't anything special." But Kaylee knew he was being modest. She also knew that since the day he had rolled that tiny soccer ball against her even tinier baby booties, he had foreseen a future where crowds cheered wildly as Kaylee O'Shay tore up the defense and wore out goalies in youth leagues, in high school, and eventually in college.

But that future would never happen.

Kaylee had begun taking Irish dance lessons last fall, and as her passion for dance grew, it began to interfere with soccer matches and practices. Eventually, dance won. The St. Patrick's Day indoor tournament at the Paavo Sport Complex six months ago had been her last soccer competition.

Kaylee knew that her father understood her decision. She had liked being coached by her father, and eventually she had become a fairly decent player. However, Tom O'Shay ultimately came to realize that she loved Irish dance in a way she would never love soccer. Kaylee suspected that her decision had created a tiny sad place inside of him, a place that would remain for a long time.

"I'm sorry I didn't see you at all last night," Kaylee's mother told her, putting the last of the clothing into a laundry basket. "You were asleep by the time I got home. How did Thursday night's dance practice go?"

Kaylee had been looking forward to the first practice in September all summer long. Based on her anxious behavior and nonstop chatter, one might have thought that Christmas Day, the first day of summer vacation, and Kaylee's next ten birthdays had all been rescheduled so that they would occur on the first Thursday in September. In fact, the date marked the start of her second year at Trean Gaoth Academy of Irish Dance.

"Awesome!" Kaylee instantly forgot the seriously twisted and quite possibly pure-evil dream, her face suddenly brightening with an inner energy that most eleven-year-olds lack just minutes after stumbling out of bed on Saturday. "We're learning new steps! Hard shoe steps!"

Beth O'Shay smiled and nodded, lifting a crock pot onto the countertop. Year two meant ear-splitting hard shoe dances would be added to the soft shoe routines her daughter already knew. Year two also meant Kaylee's first feis, which was what Irish dance competitions were called.

First-year dancers wore black, ballet-style soft shoes, called ghillies. In these, the first years learned dances that required athletic precision, the concentration of a gymnast and the heart of an artist.

Beautiful dances.

Second years learned the hard shoe steps as well, which led to routines that were breathtaking, dynamic and loud.

Exciting dances.

"You'll have to show me your new steps later," Beth O'Shay said, sprinkling bread crumbs onto ground beef she had placed in a large mixing bowl moments earlier.

Kaylee bounced up from the table. "I can show you now!" She started to dance, but stopped after a few moments when her grandmother bustled into the kitchen to demand Mrs. O'Shay's attention.

"Bethany, where's my purse?" asked Grandma Birdsall, who had come to live with Kaylee's family a little more than two years earlier.

"I'm sure it's wherever you left it, Mom," Kaylee's mother said.

"Well," said the old woman, visibly flustered, "I've got to find it. I have an appointment with Dr. Holland this morning!"

"We'll find it, Mom." Mrs. O'Shay turned to Kaylee, her face a mixture of resignation and pleading. "Honey, go change into some clothes. We'll have to leave for Grandma's appointment in a little while."

Kaylee looked down at her sweatpants and t-shirt, feeling the pleasant laziness of the morning begin to evaporate. "Why can't I wear these?"

Kaylee's mother flashed her daughter an exasperated look. "Kaylee, you slept in those!"

"Bethany," pressed Grandma Birdsall, "what about my purse?"

Before Mrs. O'Shay could answer, loud footsteps sounded and Will in full soccer regalia bounded down the stairs from his room, an open box of cinnamon-flavored breakfast cereal under his arm. Right behind was Tom O'Shay, a slim man with thinning brown hair and gentle, hazel eyes. He rushed over and planted a kiss on his wife's cheek.

"See you around lunch time!" he called, and followed his son toward the door to the garage.

Mrs. O'Shay wrinkled her nose at her husband. "Why are you leaving so early? Isn't your practice at nine o'clock?"

Tom O'Shay nodded as he backed toward the door. "That gives us about ten minutes!" Then he frowned. "Shouldn't you be leaving about this time, too?" With a wave, he disappeared out the door.

Beth O'Shay snapped her wrist to eye level and examined her watch. "Oh, shoot! This old thing is stopped again! Kaylee, grab some shorts! You can change in the car!"

Grandma Birdsall waved her hands helplessly. "But my purse . . ."

"We'll find it, Mom!" said Mrs. O'Shay, now moving like a mother hurricane.

"Are you sure I have to come?" whined Kaylee, reluctantly leaving the table.

"I have to open the store at nine!" cried her mother, placing the top on the crock pot and hurriedly washing her hands in the sink. "And your grandmother isn't very steady on her feet. She needs someone to help her. Oh, we're going to be late!"

Kaylee hesitated. "But I wanted to—"

"Kaylee, don't argue!" said Beth O'Shay, attempting to control her voice. "Please, just get in the car! Now!"

The dream was working. Her day was becoming horrid. Kaylee ran to her room, grabbed a clean t-shirt from her dresser and a pair of shorts from the floor—shorts that would pass for clean if not inspected too closely. She snatched up her shoes on the way to the door, and in a moment, the three of them were pinned against the seats as Mrs. O'Shay accelerated down Cranberry Street.

Her father breezing off to soccer without her.

Everyone rushing around like crazy.

No parachuting into the mouth of an open volcano.

Life as usual at the O'Shay house.

Two

While her mother sped toward downtown Rosemary as if she were a driver in the Indianapolis 500, Kaylee slipped on the shorts and her favorite top, a pale green t-shirt featuring an illustration of ghillies and the words LOVE THE DANCE above TREAN GAOTH ACADEMY OF IRISH DANCE. It had rained during the night, but the morning beamed cheery sunlight at them, reminding Kaylee that she would have to enjoy it through a window until her father rescued her from grandma duty at noon.

Mrs. O'Shay dropped off Kaylee and Grandma Birdsall in front of Dr. Holland's office, which sat a little more than a block south of Mrs. O'Shay's shop. "You're just a couple minutes late," she said as Grandma Birdsall made her slow-motion exit from the vehicle. "Hopefully they won't make you reschedule." Then she sped off to open up the Stitchin' Kitchen, her combination fabric store and coffee shop that had been struggling along for almost three years.

Grandma Birdsall—short and thin with white hair—shuffled across the sidewalk to the front door of the building, which had been remodeled with lots of glass and fake brick and pastel colors so that it no longer looked like it belonged with the other buildings in the downtown area. She moved awkwardly, avoiding a muddy-looking puddle that had formed in a low spot. Kaylee's grandmother used a cane to steady herself ever since she had passed out unexpectedly last spring. The doctors had diagnosed a heart condition and had prescribed a daily buffet of enormous pills. Today's appointment was some sort of check-up related to that.

The fainting spell had badly scared Kaylee, and afterwards she had made a promise to herself to be nicer to her grandmother—a promise she sometimes found difficult to keep. It seemed like her grandmother always wanted Kaylee to help her with something, and this *always* seemed to occur when Kaylee wanted to be doing something completely different—and much more fun. And with her grandmother living in the house, there were certain times when Kaylee couldn't invite friends to come over because Grandma had plans, or couldn't go off riding her bicycle because someone had to stay with Grandma, or couldn't be so loud because Grandma was sleeping.

On the other hand, she really loved Grandma Birdsall and enjoyed the sewing projects they worked on together.

"They probably won't see me today," fretted Grandma Birdsall as Kaylee held the heavy glass door open. "Everything I need is in my purse!" Mrs. O'Shay had assured them that the doctor already had Grandma's insurance information, so the purse would not matter. It was clear to Kaylee, however, that her grandmother could not imagine any successful encounter with another human being that did not include her big, black handbag.

"It'll be okay, Grandma," said Kaylee patiently.

As her grandmother continued to take forever to maneuver herself through the doorway, two girls wearing inline skates, green soccer jerseys and small backpacks whizzed past Kaylee's elbow, probably on their way to a morning game at Kennedy Park. Kaylee instinctively turned in their direction just as they hit the nearby puddle, which sent a small spray of brown water onto her. The two girls skidded to a halt a few sidewalk squares away. "Hey!" called one of the girls. "It's O'Shrimp!"

It was Brittany Hall and Heather Chandler, two of the best players from her old soccer team—and, as far as Kaylee was concerned, two of the nastiest. Kaylee had no idea why Brittany disliked her so, but Kaylee had been harassed by her ever since their first year together on the team. Heather automatically joined in on anything that Brittany did.

"I can see why you quit soccer," said Brittany, looking past Kaylee to where her grandmother moved unsteadily through the doorway. "You're so much better as a door-holder!"

"It's our first game of the season," said Heather. "And without you, we might actually have a chance of *winning*!"

Brittany grinned as if she had just pulled the first wing off a fly. "Now that we've gotten rid of half of the losers on the team, maybe we'll be good!"

Kaylee knew that the other "loser" Brittany was referring to was Jackie Kizobu, Kaylee's best friend on the Green Storm. Jackie loved soccer, but was nowhere near as talented as Brittany or Heather. Kaylee tried to think of some clever comeback that would make her two, obnoxious, former teammates feel like dirt. Before she could, Heather made a face like she had smelled garbage and asked, "What's a Train Goth?"

"It's pronounced TRY-an GAY-uth," said Kaylee, glancing down at the navy blue letters. "And it means— " She was unable to utter the words *strong wind*, her mouth suddenly stuck in the open position as she saw the brown flecks of puddle water spattered across her favorite top.

"My shirt!" cried Kaylee, using both hands to try and brush the muddy spots off. From behind, her grandmother uttered a panicky little shout.

"Kaylee!"

She turned in horror to see her grandmother sprawled on the floor. Kaylee realized that she had let go of the heavy door. Her grandmother's shoe had become caught when it closed on her. Blood seeped from a cut in Grandma Birdsall's knee.

Dr. Holland's receptionist had already rushed forward to help.

"O'Shrimp, you are a complete klutz!" said Brittany, starting down the sidewalk. Heather threw back her head in laughter and followed.

*

Beth O'Shay had been livid. She had smiled at Kaylee and Grandma Birdsall when they arrived at the Stitchin' Kitchen. "My, that appointment certainly took longer than I expected." Then she had spotted the bandage on her mother's knee and another on her forearm.

The smile had disappeared.

Three stitches on the knee. A few scrapes on the elbow. "And a tetanus shot," Grandma Birdsall had noted proudly, pointing at her shoulder.

Kaylee had felt awful. She had managed to hold back the tears in the doctor's office as they patched up Grandma Birdsall, but it had been a struggle. Dr. Holland had seemed to sense this and had patted her on the head. "Darned old heavy door. Maybe it's time I installed one of those buttons that opens it automatically."

On the walk to the Stitchin' Kitchen, Kaylee had told herself that she would not cry when she was explaining things to her mother. However, as Beth O'Shay's eyes widened when she first spotted the bandages, the saltwater began to spill. It did not stop until many hugs had been administered by Kaylee's mother and Grandma Birdsall.

"When I put you in charge of your grandmother, you have to take that responsibility seriously, dear,"

Beth O'Shay said gently. "She's not as steady on her feet as she used to be."

After that, Kaylee's mother turned her attention to two older women on sewing machines near the front of the store. Kaylee felt better as a result of the hugs, but she did not look forward to the next hour and a half doing nothing at the Stitchin' Kitchen until her father and Will picked her up on their way home from soccer. She could have walked the distance, but she knew that her mother would not be pleased if she abandoned Grandma Birdsall. Especially after what had happened today.

The Stitchin' Kitchen was Beth O'Shay's dream, a store crammed full of fabric bolts, patterns, threads, samples and sewing supplies. However, it was the coffee bar near the entrance that made the Stitchin' Kitchen different from other fabric stores. Kaylee's mother had noticed coffee bars inside stores that sold music, books and even art supplies. "Why not in a fabric store?" she had reasoned. "Lots of women like to sew, and they like good coffee, too. Here they can have both." Several sewing machines formed an arc near the coffee bar, and Beth O'Shay taught lessons on these. When Kaylee visited the store, her mother would sometimes make her a mocha cappuccino with extra whipped cream.

Grandma Birdsall settled behind the machine farthest away from the two women being supervised by her daughter. Kaylee found a chair nearby and pawed a book from her back pocket, a story about a girl gymnast who volunteered at a vet's office while secretly training to be an astronaut. *I wish someone would write a book about Irish dancing,* she sighed.

After a page or two, she felt someone kiss her on the top of her head. She looked up from the book to see her mother smiling over her shoulder as she returned to the women near the bar. Kaylee noticed that a mocha cappuccino with extra whipped cream had appeared in front of her. She took a sip. The Saturday morning improved slightly.

"You're so quiet," said Grandma Birdsall, who Kaylee noticed was sewing the zipper into some sort of long coat. "I hope you're not still feeling sad. I'm just fine, really."

Kaylee did not know what to say to this. Brittany and Heather tormented her constantly. Her father spent all his time with Will. Her mother's store was losing money. She couldn't do any of the cool things she wanted to do on this Saturday morning. Her favorite t-shirt had muddy stains on the front. And she had almost killed her grandmother. *Oh yes, I should just be doing happy somersaults all around the store.*

Grandma Birdsall seemed to sense Kaylee's despair. She stopped her machine and squinted at her granddaughter's t-shirt. "We might be able to get those stains out. Go get your other top from the car."

After retrieving the slept-in t-shirt, Kaylee followed her grandmother to the small bathroom at the back of the store. As she changed back into the spare shirt, Grandma Birdsall put a rubber stopper in the old sink, dispensed some hand soap from a plastic container, and made a foamy broth. She kneaded Kaylee's green shirt into this for several minutes and then motioned for them to return to their seats. "We'll let it soak. Hopefully the stains haven't set."

Kaylee sighed and kissed her grandmother on the temple. She felt guiltier than ever about almost killing her. "I don't know why you're so nice to me."

"It's part of the rules of grandmothering," said the old woman brightly. "And I also do it because you're a very special little lady, Kaylee."

Kaylee blushed slightly. "All grandmas think their grandkids are special."

"That's true," nodded Grandma Birdsall. "But in your case, I have proof of how special you are. You don't remember your Grandpa Joey."

"He died before I was born," said Kaylee. Grandpa Joey had been Grandma Birdsall's first husband. From what Kaylee had been told, he was a wiry little jokester with a kind word and a smile for everyone. Kaylee's only memory was of Grandpa Birdsall, her grandmother's second husband who had passed away when Kaylee was five.

"Actually," said Grandma Birdsall, "Grandpa Joey died in a car accident the week *after* you were born. You may not remember him, but *he* met *you.* When your mother brought you home from the hospital, he lifted you into the air and said, 'I'm not rich. For right now, this kiss will have to do for a birthday gift!' Then he gave you one right on your little forehead. He said, 'It's a kiss full of blessings! A life full of blessings for my little Kaylee!'"

Her grandmother sat back, a satisfied look on her face as if this story should wash away all the sorrow in Kaylee's life. Kaylee managed a weak smile. Inside, however, she felt far from blessed. Grandpa Joey's story had reminded her of a bit of lore from her father's side of the family tree that he often mentioned. Tom O'Shay had told his daughter that all the O'Shays had to stay short because Great-Great-Grandpa O'Shay gambled away his fortune, and when he built the family's ancestral home in Ireland, he could only afford enough wood to make the ceiling five feet ten inches tall.

Instead of feeling blessed, Kaylee felt double-cursed.

On her father's side, cursed with shortness.

On her mother's side, her grandfather had croaked a couple of days after kissing her.

So much for the luck of the Irish.

Three

"Cereal for lunch?" Kaylee asked her brother after listening to him eat for a few moments. A reply grunt from Will, while unintelligible, seemed to suggest that yes, cereal was the perfect food for any occasion.

The sugary corn clusters disappeared at an alarming rate and at an even more alarming decibel level. Kaylee—still feeling guilty about nearly killing her grandmother the previous day, and also feeling grouchy at having wasted a perfectly good Saturday—opened her mouth to offer Will advice on table manners that she hoped would spread her grouchy mood to him, but thought better of it when Tom O'Shay strode into the kitchen.

"We're out of here!" he said brightly. On this particular Sunday afternoon he wore the dark-blue warm-up suit that indicated he would be coaching soccer.

Since he no longer coached the team that Kaylee had played on the previous year, he had agreed to coach Will's team, the Bullets. Jackie Kizobu's father had taken over coaching duties on the Green Storm.

Tom O'Shay leaned over and kissed Kaylee on the head. Then he patted Will's shoulder affectionately. "Let's move it, boy. Don't want to be late. We're playing the Avalanche today!"

Will tipped the bowl into his face, drained it in one final, obscene mega-slurp, and left it rattling noisily on the tabletop as he followed his father out the door.

Kaylee watched them go and sighed, moving to the refrigerator to find meat for a sandwich for her own lunch. On the plus side, Kaylee did not have to hurry after church on Sundays. Her mother had to rush to get to the Stitchin' Kitchen, which was open from noon to four. Her father and Will usually raced off to an early afternoon soccer game. Kaylee could take her time with lunch.

On the minus side, she missed the excitement of getting ready for a big game. She missed spending time with her former teammates. Well, *some* of them. Most of all, she missed spending time with her father.

Noticing that Kaylee's Sunday afternoons were free, Grandma Birdsall had stepped in and offered sewing lessons. Kaylee often had trouble deciding whether this was a blessing or a curse. Sitting in her grandmother's room—cluttered with knick-knacks, sewing machines, boxes and fabric samples—was not the most exciting way to spend a Sunday afternoon, and Kaylee often found herself guiltily wishing that her grandmother might forget or be feeling under the weather.

On the other hand, Kaylee usually discovered that she enjoyed whatever activity her grandmother had planned. She also enjoyed Grandma Birdsall's stories about Grandpa Joey or the big house where she had lived with Grandpa Birdsall. Kaylee remembered the house, the smell of Thanksgiving dinners coming from its kitchen, the enormous closets upstairs where she and Will played hide-n-seek, the apple tree in the backyard that was perfect for climbing.

Kaylee's additions to the conversations often focused on Irish dance, and she would frequently pop up from whatever she was sewing to demonstrate a step for her grandmother.

This particular Sunday, as Kaylee struggled to properly align the squares on a section of quilt, she babbled on about the same thing she had been babbling on about all summer: her first feis.

"It's going to be so awesome!" said Kaylee, who unlike her grandmother, had difficulty talking and sewing at the same time. As a result, Kaylee usually accomplished far less than anticipated during their hour together. "I might get to do my hornpipe," she added, referring to one of the hard shoe dances. Then she popped up and demonstrated the steps to her grandmother, who paused to watch proudly.

Kaylee made a frustrated face. "It's better when you're wearing hard shoes."

Grandma Birdsall marveled at Kaylee, who was not even breathing hard after performing the lightning-fast footwork.

"Annie's newsletter said there would be used hard shoes for sale at next Thursday's practice," said Kaylee. Annie Delaney was the owner of Trean Gaoth Academy of Irish Dance and one of Kaylee's dance teachers. "It'll be so cool to have a pair!"

Kaylee would have loved owning a brand-new pair of hard shoes, but money was tight at the O'Shay house. Her father, who worked at the hardware store in Rosemary, sometimes joked that if they doubled his salary, he could afford to be poor. Her mother's store, the Stitchin' Kitchen, had earned a loyal and appreciative clientele, but the cash required to run the business often exceeded what Beth O'Shay made in sales. These financial realities put the O'Shay parents in a tough spot: How do you allow your children to chase their dreams when you're broke?

Her brother Will needed money for soccer leagues and uniforms and spikes. Kaylee's dance lessons were expensive, but the costs of Irish dancing didn't end there. There were two kinds of shoes, special socks, headbands and a Trean Gaoth school dress. Luckily, Grandma Birdsall had helped with some of that. She had secretly paid for Kaylee's lessons the first year, and had sewn the gorgeous navy-and-gold school dress that otherwise would have cost hundreds of dollars.

"So," said Grandma Birdsall as Kaylee settled back behind her machine, "when is your first feis?"

"Caitlin says there's one in Chicago in January," said Kaylee. Caitlin Hubbard lived in Paavo--about ten miles from Kaylee's home in Rosemary--and was Kaylee's closest friend at the dance school. "She thinks there will be more than two thousand girls at it!"

Her grandmother nodded. "But you won't compete against all of them. Only the girls who are in your age group."

"Caitlin says the best dancers get medals," Kaylee said breathlessly. "Do you think I'll get a medal?"

Grandma Birdsall laughed. "I think you'll have fun. That's what's important."

The doorbell interrupted them. Kaylee jogged to the front door and found Jackie Kizobu standing in front of her parked bicycle.

"How'd the game go yesterday?" asked Kaylee, holding open the door for her friend.

"We tied, 1-1. Brittany and Heather blamed it on you." Jackie was of Asian heritage, skinny, and had a playground of braces on her teeth.

Kaylee scrunched up her face. "How can they blame me? I'm not even on the team anymore!"

"Brittany said that she and Heather ran into you on the way to the game," Jackie explained. "Said seeing you jinxed them."

Kaylee unloaded an exasperated sigh as she rounded the corner in front of her grandmother's room. "Seeing them wasn't very lucky for me, either. They almost ruined my favorite shirt!"

"And your favorite grandmother!" cried Grandma Birdsall as the two girls bubbled into the room. "Why Jackie, it's been ages! We hardly ever see you anymore!"

"I've been busy with flute lessons and soccer," said Jackie. "I played three-on-three tournaments all summer."

"I didn't know they had three-on-three tournaments for flute," said Grandma Birdsall.

Jackie mouth dropped open, and after a short pause, Grandma Birdsall smiled slyly. "Just a little joke, dear." Once Jackie understood that Kaylee's grandmother was joking and not losing her mind, she laughed. Then Grandma Birdsall shooed them out of her room. "Go spend some time together. Kaylee and I can sew anytime!"

Kaylee hugged her grandmother and scurried off across the hall with Jackie.

"Zizzers, it really has been a long time since I was in your room," said Jackie. "I can actually see your floor! It must have taken months for you to clean up all the t-shirts and underwear!"

Kaylee found a pair of underpants that had not been rescued from the floor and fired a perfect shot into Jackie's face. Since she had started Irish dance, Kaylee kept the floor of her room fairly clean, if fairly clean could be defined as fewer than ten rumpled items of clothing. She had not suddenly become a neat-freak. It was simply easier to practice her dance steps if she didn't have to worry about tripping over piles of dirty laundry.

"So did you score the goal in yesterday's game?" Kaylee asked her friend.

Jackie rolled her eyes and flopped onto Kaylee's day bed. "Are you kidding? I haven't gotten a shot since you quit the team. No one else ever passes me the ball!"

Kaylee sat on the floor with her back against the wall. "They're idiots."

"I wish you were still on the Green Storm," Jackie sighed.

Kaylee thought about saying "me too," but couldn't quite get the words to come out.

"Yeah, if you were still on the team," continued Jackie, "Brittany would probably forget all about me and go back to harassing you.

Kaylee found another pair of underpants and lobbed these at Jackie, landing them atop her head. As memories of Brittany's cruelties clattered through her brain, a more pleasant vision appeared as well.

"Do a lot of the sixth-grade boys come to watch your games?" asked Kaylee.

Jackie smiled wickedly. "Oh, not many. Usually only one. Now let me see, who might it be? I have such a bad memory."

"Stop it!" said Kaylee, finding a third pair of underwear sticking partly out from under her dresser and hitting Jackie with it right between the eyes.

"Zizzers, you must not have any clean underwear left!" said Jackie. "But if you must know, Michael Black still follows Brittany around like a puppy on a leash."

Michael Black was the cutest boy in the sixth grade.

"I don't like Michael Black," Kaylee said vehemently. "I've just never been able to figure out why he hangs around with a creep like Brittany. She's so mean to everyone!"

"I think it has something to do with the fact that she's got massive fat deposits in all the places that sixth grade boys enjoy seeing massive fat deposits," said Jackie. "You and me, we've got about as many fat deposits as a couple of celery sticks."

"My mom said she's mature for her age," said Kaylee.

"She's a chunk, all right," agreed Jackie. "So if you want to steal Michael Black away from her, you'd better start eating double desserts."

"I don't like Michael Black!" repeated Kaylee.

"Sure," nodded Jackie indulgently. "And I don't like Angelo Zizzo." The walls of Jackie's room were plastered with posters of the Italian soccer star. As evidence of her obsession, Jackie had recently begun saying "Zizzers!" whenever she was especially excited about something. "Hey!" Jackie cried suddenly, remembering the TV in Kaylee's room. "Let's check out the sports channels! There may be a soccer match on!"

"I'm the only kid in Rosemary whose family doesn't have cable, remember?" said Kaylee dully.

"Oh yeah," said Jackie, who went on to narrate the Angelo Zizzo-highlights of the last game played by the Italians. By the time she was finished, Kaylee almost felt like she had seen it on one of the sports channels. They were silent again for a few moments until Jackie spoke.

"Sixth grade is going to be a great year!"

Kaylee nodded. Dancing in her first feis would make it great, although she was pretty certain that was not what Jackie had meant.

"We're the oldest kids at the school," explained Jackie. "So we'll be in charge of everything! And this year, we get to go to dances!"

Well, thought Kaylee, *at least we were both thinking about dance.* She knew, however, that Jackie was referring to dances where a deejay would play music in the middle school gymnasium while colorful strobe lights flashed. And there would be boys.

"Yup, it's going to be great!" repeated Jackie. "Hey, let's make plans for this week! Ask your parents if you can go see a movie in Paavo on Thursday!"

Kaylee was about to say that it sounded like a great idea, but then she remembered dance class.

"I know," said Kaylee. "Let's have a sleepover on Friday!"

Jackie made an injured face. "I don't think my dad will let me. There's a game Saturday morning, and he doesn't want me up until four in the morning before a soccer game. There's a game on Sunday, too."

"Tell him we'll only stay up until two," said Kaylee, and both girls laughed.

"Maybe we can do something the following week," suggested Jackie.

Kaylee smiled. "Yeah." Then her face lit up. "Hey, I've got something to show you!"

Jackie sat up on the bed, her face expectant. "What?"

Kaylee popped to her feet. "My new steps!" She danced through her hornpipe, finishing with a perfect bow.

Jackie nodded slowly. "That's pretty cool."

"It's better with music," Kaylee said awkwardly. "And shoes. With hard shoes it sounds really cool!"

"I'll bet," said Jackie, hopping off the bed. "I gotta go. I'll see you in school tomorrow!"

Kaylee followed her friend to the front door, where Jackie turned and gave her a hug. "Really miss you at soccer!"

"Me too," said Kaylee, and then she watched her ride off down Cranberry Street on her bicycle.

Four

The Golden Academy of Irish Dance often made visitors gasp. In sixteen years, the studio on the west side of Milwaukee had grown from eighty dancers to more than one thousand. After several lavish construction projects, Golden was now considered "the most impressive facility for the teaching of Irish dance in the Midwest" according to its own brochure. The academy featured a large gym, half a dozen smaller dance studios, a modern weight room, a training and medical room, a small therapy pool, offices for director Clarissa Golden—whose father, owner of a chain of clothing stores, had bankrolled the facilities upgrade—and her staff, not to mention a 100-seat theater where dancers could hold meetings or critique films of themselves.

And there was a juice bar situated in a beautiful glass-walled atrium.

Dancers from Golden had appeared on television shows, in magazines and even in a recent popular movie—although only for about forty seconds. Not only that, it was difficult to find a feis in the Midwest where girls from Golden Academy were not vying for first place. Several, in fact, had won individual World titles.

"Our mission at Golden Academy, is the same as our motto," the brochure quoted owner Clarissa Golden. "To be 'simply the best'!"

Kaylee O'Shay did not belong to the Golden Academy team. She took her lessons at Trean Gaoth Academy of Irish Dance, located a bit more than half an hour west of Golden Academy in the town of Paavo. Instead of a cutting-edge architectural marvel of a dance studio, Trean Gaoth's three hundred dancers trained in a renovated bowling alley. A vast dance floor had been built over the eight lanes. The former bar area had been partitioned into offices for Annie Delaney's staff.

"Do you ever wonder what it would be like to dance for Golden?" Kaylee asked her friend Caitlin as the two laced up their ghillies for the first Thursday practice in October.

"It would be awful," replied Caitlin, a look of disgust on her face. "I could never keep my nose in the air for as long as they do!"

Kaylee laughed, pulling her poodle socks tight. "They aren't really that stuck-up, are they?"

Caitlin shrugged. "Your friend Brittany seems to be."

Kaylee had to admit that this was a good point. Brittany had made it her personal mission to torment Kaylee at every opportunity. She recalled the soccer diva's seething remarks last winter after Kaylee had passed the ball to Jackie instead of Brittany for the winning shot against one of the league's top teams, the Lasers. *I'll remember that, O'Shay!* Brittany had growled at her. *It was a close game and you had a choice between Jackie and me. No one with an ounce of brains would have passed it to someone like her if they could have passed it to a really good player.*

While it was true that Jackie Kizobu was not exactly a scoring machine, Brittany had been covered by two Laser players. Jackie had made the shot—her first-ever goal—and the Green Storm had won the game. Still, Brittany had been furious.

If anyone other than your daddy was coaching this team, you'd be sitting on the sidelines. Making stupid passes to your favorites rather than doing what's best for the team. What a loser.

Of course, now Kaylee had given up soccer so that she could devote more of her energies to Irish dance. Unfortunately, this did not rid her of Brittany Hall.

Brittany danced for Golden Academy.

"Do you think all the girls at Golden are like Brittany?" asked Kaylee as she and her friend pushed themselves to their feet and started toward the center of the vast dance floor.

"Absolutely!" said Caitlin. "Some people just have defective genes. I read about it in the newspaper. People with good genes become doctors or teachers or firemen. People with bad genes become burglars or join Golden Academy or become clowns."

Kaylee appeared astonished. "Clowns?"

Caitlin nodded. "Clowns have always scared me. I think they're evil."

Both girls laughed. They did not laugh often during the next hour and a half. Tara and Miss Helen, the two instructors, worked the twenty-five girls in the class the way drill sergeants would work Marine recruits. With only three months until the first feisanna of the new year, there was still much work to be done.

The two friends crawled to their water bottles after practice, but Annie Delaney, tall with long gold hair tied back in a ponytail, emerged from her office and summoned the girls back to the center of the dance floor where they sat in a semi-circle. "Some of you will be entering a feis for the first time this year," said Annie in a tone that suggested this was a significant milestone. Then she held up a stack of papers. "This handout contains the address of web sites where your parents can learn which feisanna are available in each state. It also contains information on two Wisconsin feises that will be coming up this winter. Feises are a lot of fun, girls. And you learn so much about yourself as a dancer."

The stack of papers circulated through the group.

"I can't wait!" said Caitlin, holding the paper in her fist triumphantly. "This is going to be so cool!"

Kaylee felt the electric excitement, too, but she also had so many questions. "I guess so. But I'm not even really sure what a feis is."

"Sure you are," said Caitlin, unlacing her ghillies. "Annie has talked about them before. A feis is a competition!"

"I know that." Kaylee nodded uncertainly while working on removing her own shoes. "But how does it work? Do we all dance together? Does everyone use the same music? How do you tell who wins and who loses?"

One of their dance instructors, Miss Helen, a woman in her fifties with unevenly graying hair and the powerful physical build of an Olympic discus thrower, caught this part of the conversation and knelt beside the two friends. She wore a plain black t-shirt and black cotton sweat pants that looked like she might have owned them for decades. Miss Helen had never seemed particularly friendly toward Kaylee, and at least part of the reason for this appeared to be Kaylee's connection to soccer, which Miss Helen hated passionately. "Why run through the mud when you can dance on the wind?" Miss Helen had once asked Kaylee.

This was shortly before Kaylee had ditched the big St. Patrick's Day dance show in order to play in a soccer tournament.

"Have either of you been to a feis?" Miss Helen asked, the unpleasant aroma of cigarettes accompanying her words.

Both girls shook their heads, and Kaylee tried to avoid wrinkling her nose at the smell.

"Feis is a Gaelic word that means festival," explained Miss Helen in her husky voice. "But today it's used most often to mean a dance and music competition. At a feis, you can enter one dance, such as the reel, but some girls enter four, five or even more dances."

"Five dances?" gasped Kaylee, forgetting the cigarette smell for a moment. "I'd be exhausted!"

Miss Helen almost smiled, a rare thing. "Yes, it can be tiring. But you don't dance them all together. They're spread out over five or six hours."

"I've heard there can be over two thousand girls at some feises," said Caitlin.

"Boys dance, too," noted Miss Helen solemnly, who then reminded them of several boys at Trean Gaoth Academy who were about their age.

"How can a judge ever watch two thousand people dance in just one day?" asked Kaylee, imagining a line of dancers stretching from the edge of their dance floor, out the front doors, through the parking lot and down Paavo's main street.

"In some feisanna," Miss Helen continued, "there are eight or ten stages, each one about thirty feet across. Each stage has a judge. Dancers are divided by age and ability. You might be dancing against fifteen or twenty other girls."

"Do all twenty dance at the same time?" asked Kaylee.

"All twenty girls are lined up along the back of the stage, facing the judge, who is usually at a table across from them," said Miss Helen patiently. "At a signal from the judge, the music starts. The first two girls step out from the group, point their toes in the ready position, and then begin their steps. The judge measures them against each other, but also against the standard of excellence for that dance. Are the toes pointed? Are the leaps high? Is she in time to the music? And so on. When the two girls finish their routine in a minute or two, they bow and exit the stage while the next two in line begin their dance. The music doesn't stop until all twenty have gone."

"Wow!" said Kaylee, finally noticing the shoes in her hand and stowing them in her duffel. "That's not how I imagined it at all!"

Miss Helen straightened and spoke like a general readying her troops for battle. "A first feis can be a little intimidating, but after that, you'll be an expert." Then she marched over to another group of seated dancers, whose conversation absorbed her immediately.

Caitlin suddenly grabbed Kaylee's forearm. "Let's do lots of feises! It'll be fun and we'll get to be really great dancers!"

"Yeah," said Kaylee, imagining herself on stage, in front of a judge, in front of hundreds of people, competing in her beautiful navy-and-gold Trean Gaoth school dress. "I can't wait!"

When her mother arrived home from the Stitchin' Kitchen later that evening, Kaylee showed her the paper containing the web sites for feis information. "You really think you're ready for this?" asked her mother, but she already knew the answer from the look on her daughter's face.

"Wow!" Kaylee's eyes widened as she and her mother scrolled down the site listing the year's feisanna. "There's so many! We could go to almost any state!"

Beth O'Shay nodded, although she did not seem as surprised as Kaylee had expected.

"Caitlin and I are going to be great dancers, Mom!" announced Kaylee, popping up and breaking into a jig behind her mother's chair. "We're going to enter lots of feises!"

Mrs. O'Shay continued to scroll the site. "It looks like they're organized by date."

"Go to January!" instructed Kaylee. "We want to do our first feis right at the start of the new year!"

Mrs. O'Shay examined the list of cities hosting feises in January. "Let's see . . . Houston, Memphis, Sacramento . . . here's one for Alberta in Canada!"

Kaylee squealed. "Let's go to Canada!"

Mrs. O'Shay half turned, gave her daughter the *Yeah, right!* look. Then she turned back to the computer screen, scrolled into February and her face brightened. "Ah! Milwaukee!"

Kaylee joined her mother, their noses inches from the monitor: *Milwaukee Snowfeis*.

"That's one Annie talked about!" said Kaylee, pointing. "Let's enter!"

Kaylee's mother clicked on the site link and a bright blue-and-white *Milwaukee Snowfeis* graphic blossomed on the screen. "They certainly make it easy for you!" said Mrs. O'Shay.

An hour and fifteen minutes later, after reading the entry form twice, calling Caitlin's mother three times for advice, running to another room to find her credit card, filling out online forms for feis registration and a special account to pay for the feis registration, calling Caitlin's mother a fourth time to make sure she had entered Kaylee in the correct dance and age categories, submitting the online form, rechecking the site to see if it confirmed that her daughter had been registered, Beth O'Shay finally announced that she absolutely felt pretty sure that Kaylee was entered in Milwaukee's Snowfeis.

"Are you sure you wouldn't rather go back to Miss Suzy's?" Mrs. O'Shay asked her daughter, referring to the local teacher of tap and ballet lessons from whom Kaylee had taken classes a few years earlier. She simultaneously began hunting in an upper cupboard for her not-so-secret stash of chocolate which was to be consumed in large doses following stressful situations.

"No way!" said Kaylee. "I liked the dance classes with Miss Suzy. But it wasn't like Irish dance." Then Kaylee looked back in the direction from which they had come. "Can't we sign up for some more feises tonight? The Milwaukee Snowfeis isn't until February!"

Beth O'Shay shook her head. "I don't have the stamina," she said, slumping into one of the kitchen chairs. Then she smiled at her daughter. "Don't worry. Now that I've got the hang of it, I'm sure the process will go smoother for the next one. But it will be awhile before I sign you up for another feis."

"Why?" asked Kaylee.

"Registration doesn't open for the next one in the area for another couple of weeks," she said. "Unless you want to go all the way to Calgary."

Kaylee made a pleading face, pulling out a second chair so that she could sit next to her mother.

"No!" said Mrs. O'Shay, laughing. "Besides, these feises are expensive. We're already paying for lessons, socks, special shoes. You're going to have to do a lot more weed pulling to earn enough for all these entry fees. And if we go to a feis that's out of state, there's gas money for the car, meals, hotel rooms. We may have to pick our feises carefully, sweetheart."

"I'll work hard," promised Kaylee. "I'll earn a lot of money."

Beth O'Shay leaned forward suddenly and hugged her daughter. "I know you will, sweetheart. You're a very hard worker." She paused, and it seemed to Kaylee as if her mother were struggling to control her voice. "I sometimes wish I had kept my teaching job," she continued. "It would be so much easier to give you the things you want, the things you really deserve. But we all have to chase our dreams, Kaylee. You know how it is, sweetheart. You make choices."

Kaylee squeezed her mother back. She knew exactly how it was.

Five

"Your workmanship is really looking very good!" said Grandma Birdsall proudly. "Pretty soon you'll be teaching *me* new tricks!"

Kaylee knew that her grandmother was just being kind. Grandma Birdsall had been sewing for all but the first five of her seventy-one years. A white-haired woman with a kind, round face, she was a real pro when it came to needle and thread. For evidence of her artistry, one needed to look no further than the beautiful Trean Gaoth school dress that she had made for her granddaughter. Most dancers purchased a school dress to wear at public performances and feisanna. The expensive costumes were specially designed and sewn for Trean Gaoth by a Chicago company.

Last year, Kaylee's parents had tried to find a reasonably priced used costume—at least that was what she had been led to believe. In reality, her grandmother, working in secret, had created a brand-new perfect copy of the Trean Gaoth school dress. "I learned most of the basic techniques for making Irish dance dresses by using the computer," Grandma Birdsall had told her later. "Why, it's amazing what you can find on the Internet!"

The dress had been intended as a Christmas present for Kaylee, but before giving it to her, Mrs. O'Shay had taken it to Annie Delaney for final approval. According to Beth O'Shay, Annie's jaw had just about knocked a hole in the floor. "Annie told me that no one had ever tried to make a school dress before," Mrs. O'Shay had proudly confessed to her daughter. "In fact, Annie told me that if anyone had asked to make one, she would have said no. The dress needed to be exact, and that's why everyone ordered them from Chicago. But when she saw the dress Mom made, well, she couldn't believe it. Said it was amazing and beautiful and it would of course be wonderful if we gave it to Kaylee."

"Just goes to show," Kaylee's father had responded, "that it's easier to ask for forgiveness than for permission. I do it all the time."

The dress certainly was amazing and beautiful, thought Kaylee. Unfortunately, her grandmother did not feel particularly amazing these days. Ever since she had passed out without warning seven months ago, it seemed that she tired more easily and sometimes found it difficult to focus on what she was doing.

"Just part of getting old," her grandmother would say, but Kaylee knew there was more to it than that and was frightened by this invisible unknown that walked stride for stride with her grandmother. After Grandma Birdsall had come to live with the O'Shay family, Kaylee had resented her presence, how she disrupted the household routine and found ways to steal away Kaylee's precious free time. Now, however, Kaylee grew cold at the thought of losing her.

"I think another Sunday or two, and this one will be done!" said Grandma Birdsall, examining her granddaughter's stitching. The project was a lap quilt, green and ivory with a big shamrock at the center. On Sunday afternoons, Kaylee used one of the three sewing machines that Grandma Birdsall kept in her room ("Each has a special purpose," her grandmother had told her) to complete the stippling, a random pattern of stitching across the face of the quilt attaching it to the backing material.

"I wish I was faster at this!" said Kaylee, her concentration riveted on the machine. Then she realized how her words might have sounded. "I don't mind spending the time with you, Grandma. I just wish I could do this as well as you can."

Grandma Birdsall smiled warmly. "You will someday. You've got a nice touch. Much better than I was at your age." Then she sighed heavily. "But that's enough for today." She helped Kaylee carefully shut down the machine. "I'm afraid I need a little nap. Silly medicines make a person tired."

As Kaylee exited her grandmother's room, she heard the slam of the door leading into the kitchen from the garage. Her father and Will tumbled into the house, laughing.

"Did you see the way I faked Brandon completely out of his socks?" Will asked his father, twirling a soccer ball on his index finger. "Man, that was wicked!"

Tom O'Shay nodded. "It was a pretty sweet move. A month ago, I don't know if you could have pulled it off."

Will tucked the ball under his elbow and opened the refrigerator door. He pulled out two sodas, handing one to his father.

"I think you and Brandon might both get some time at the forward position in next week's game," said Mr. O'Shay.

Will looked surprised. "Really?"

"Right now," explained his father, "you're the two best ball handlers I've got. Might be interesting to see both of you up front at the same time. Might be scary, as a matter of fact."

Will grinned. "Thanks, Dad!"

They took long swigs of soda and then spied Kaylee for the first time.

"Hi, sweetheart!" called her father.

Kaylee offered a tiny wave and then disappeared into her room.

She suddenly felt sort of deflated. She danced a bit of her reel, and this helped. Not completely, but somewhat. She pawed through the clutter on her desk and dug out her favorite DVD, *Isle of Green Fire*, a two-hour Irish dance spectacular with incredible music and super-cool costumes. Watching the best Irish dancers in the world, dreaming herself into their ghillies, always made her feel better.

Monday's march through the valley of the sixth grade did not brighten her outlook. At lunch, she complained gloomily to Jackie, who seemed to be in an unusually sullen mood herself. "Sometimes I wish I hadn't quit soccer," Kaylee said. "But there would have been a lot of conflicts with dance. And it would have gotten worse as I got older."

Jackie, whose straight dark hair fell to the middle of her back, used a plastic fork to stir the sliced carrots that she had deposited in her applesauce. "You know what's gotten worse? Brittany Hall. Remember how I told you that she never kicked the ball to me? Well, this last game, she did!"

"Oh," said Kaylee, stunned. "Maybe she's starting to realize that you're a pretty good player."

"You don't understand," said Jackie. "I was sitting on the bench at the time. She kicked it right at my head!"

"How do you survive?" asked Kaylee, feeling an overwhelming wave of pity for her friend.

Jackie planted an elbow on the table top and leaned her head onto a hand. "I just let my eyes glaze over and imagine Angelo Zizzo running toward me with his jersey off." In addition to her bedroom shrine to Italian professional soccer player Angelo Zizzo, Jackie had plastered the inside of her school locker—as well as all of her notebooks and folders—with pictures of the

Italian soccer star clipped from sports magazines. "Then I imagine him booting a soccer ball right into Brittany's big mouth."

Kaylee smiled, and she felt the weight of Monday lighten just a bit. "Whenever I'm bummed, you're always there for me, Jackie!"

Her friend's head slipped off her hand and she stuck out her lower lip in a pout. "I wish I could say the same thing."

"What do you mean?" asked Kaylee, surprised. "We were together yesterday afternoon!"

Jackie made a buzzing sound with her lips. "Only because *I* biked to *your* house. When was the last time *you* came over to *my* house?"

Kaylee thought for a moment. "I don't know. But come on, Jackie, we sit together every day at lunch and—"

"And that's about all," said Jackie, absent-mindedly spooning the carrot-applesauce mixture into her milk carton, whose top she had opened all the way across. "I never see you outside of school anymore. It's always 'I've got Irish dance practice' or 'We've got an Irish dance performance in Milwaukee' or 'I have to go shopping with my Irish dance girlfriends to buy Irish dance underwear'!"

"What about the sleepover where we laid on sleeping bags in the backyard and watched the meteor shower?" countered Kaylee.

"That was more than two months ago!" said Jackie, adding leftover chocolate pudding and macaroni noodles to the carton. "And you spent half the time talking about Irish dancing! What's so special about it anyway?"

"It's cool," said Kaylee, fumbling for the right words to describe her passion. "It's exciting."

Jackie shook her head. "Soccer is exciting! Soccer is cool! Dancing is so . . . so girlish!"

"I *am* a girl!" said Kaylee belligerently. "And boys do Irish dancing, too!"

"Right!" said Jackie with a snort. "There's like, what? Five boys in the Midwest who Irish dance?"

Kaylee did not want to fight with her friend, but Jackie's attitude made her angry. Kaylee had never seen her this way. A few other students seated nearby now turned their heads in the direction of the girls' argument.

"Let's not talk about this," said Kaylee, trying to lower her voice. "You're being a real pain."

"Maybe I should leave," said Jackie, lowering her own voice slightly. "Maybe I should go sit with Brittany Hall!"

"You can't stand Brittany," said Kaylee in a powerful whisper.

"Maybe not," said Jackie, "but lately, I see her more often than I see you!"

With that, Jackie took her tray to the trash cans. She did not go to sit with Brittany Hall, but she did not come back to Kaylee's table, either. Instead she stood with one shoulder against the wall, glowering at the nearby cafeteria exit, probably imagining Angelo Zizzo coming through the double doors with his shirt off in flagrant violation of the school dress code.

Kaylee felt a pang of guilt. Even though she did not want to admit it, she knew there was some truth to what Jackie had said. As she started to push herself out of her seat to go to her friend, a familiar voice brayed behind her.

"Ooh!" said Brittany, pretending to be shocked, unable to keep the broad smile from her face as she headed for the trash cans. Michael Black stood next to her, obediently carrying her mostly empty tray. "It's my favorite TV show: 'When Nerds Argue'!"

"Go away, Brittany!" said Kaylee, anger replacing her guilt in a heartbeat.

"The home audience has voted," continued Brittany, ignoring Kaylee's threat. "You're both losers!"

Kaylee had never felt such dislike for another human being. Out of the corner of her eye, she spied Jackie's abandoned milk carton on the table. Before anyone could react, she grabbed it and poured the slop over Brittany's head. Michael stood as if paralyzed, his mouth hanging open, watching the soupy sludge ooze down the sides of Brittany's head.

The sounds that came from Brittany could not quite be described as screams or words, but may perhaps have been some sort of vulgar hybrid. Even though they resisted the traditional definition of words, Kaylee knew venom and mortal embarrassment when she heard it. The sounds somehow seemed to cast the first rays of sunshine on what had otherwise been a pretty grim day.

Then the clouds returned. Deep, bruise-colored storm clouds.

"Miss O'Shay," said Principal Stone, who appeared suddenly at her left, "I'd like you to come with me!"

Six

"This is great, just great!" said an exasperated Tom O'Shay, leaning against the kitchen counter while addressing his daughter who was slumped in a chair. "I can't believe you would do something like that. I know that you and Brittany don't get along, but—"

"She treat's me like dirt, Dad," interrupted Kaylee hotly. "She's a—"

Kaylee stopped as her father cocked his head in a kind of warning.

"A big-mouthed creep," said Kaylee, somewhat less passionately. "She harasses me constantly!"

"No matter what she does, it's no excuse for fighting in school," said Tom O'Shay.

"It wasn't a fight," argued Kaylee. "I dumped crud on her."

"Whatever it was, it was the wrong way to handle the situation," said her father.

No TV, no telephone, extra chores for a week. That had been the punishment. This was in addition to the week's worth of lunch detentions she had received from Principal Stone. "And," her father had added, "you will write a letter of apology to Brittany."

Kaylee had protested. "But Dad . . ."

Her father would hear no complaints. "Next time you have a problem with somebody, you just walk away."

That seems to have been the cause of all my troubles, thought Kaylee as she sat in her room later. *I walked away from soccer, I walked away from my best friend . . .*

On Thursday at dance, she narrated the cafeteria episode to Caitlin.

"What has that girl got against you?" asked Caitlin during a water break. "Last year when your dad moved you to forward in place of her, maybe that made her angry."

"Of course it made her angry," said Kaylee. "But she started harassing me the first day she saw me."

Caitlin gave the matter a few more moments of thought. "You didn't steal her boyfriend, did you?"

I wish, thought Kaylee, but to Caitlin she said, "Of course not! Michael Black is . . ."

"Hot?" suggested Caitlin with a wide smile and a wicked twinkle in her eye.

"Not interested in girls like me," Kaylee corrected her.

"Really?" asked Caitlin coyly. "So just what kind of girl do you think you are?"

"A nerdy one," sighed Kaylee. "Just like Brittany said."

Caitlin smiled slyly. "I can't believe you would pour slop over a girl's head just because she told the truth!"

Kaylee laughed. This was why she liked Caitlin so much. Caitlin could make her smile even when they were talking about nasty things, like Brittany Hall. In that way she was a lot like . . .

A lot like Jackie.

After the break, Tara and Miss Helen worked them through their hornpipe, one of their hard shoe dances.

And bang and bang one-two step in one-two hop back one-two hop back heel slide bang and one-two hop back one-two hop back . . .

Their shoes cracked against the stage like hammers, fast and perfectly in time. Kaylee loved being inside of the percussion.

At the end of practice, Annie stood in the middle of their stretching circle. "Every year, Trean Gaoth is invited to dance for the Christmas party at Prairieland Country Club," she began. "Most of you were first-year dancers last fall, and so you were not far enough along to participate. However, now you're experienced second-year dancers!"

She paused as many of the girls acknowledged this milestone with broad smiles.

"We will be recruiting two groups of girls," continued Annie. "One will be older dancers. They will dance three or four numbers, and I'll be teaching them the routines. The other group will be younger dancers like yourselves, who will dance two or three times. We'll need twelve younger dancers from this class and the one that meets on Tuesday. Tara and Miss Helen will be in charge of your training. I have a handout here that gives the date and other important details. But it's very important that you let me know by next week if that date will work for you. We'll be picking the performing group from dancers who are not busy on that date."

Annie distributed a sheet to each girl, and then she retreated to her office.

"You've *got* to make sure you're free on this date!" squealed Caitlin as they made their way back to their street shoes. "Some of the older girls were talking about this last year. Prairieland Country Club is super-beautiful and super-rich! Everyone watching the show will be a millionaire! And they feed the dancers after the show, and it's the most delicious food ever!"

Prairieland Country Club. Kaylee had never thought she would see the inside of that exclusive sanctuary. She had heard stories about its scenic 18-

hole golf course, its oak-paneled ballroom and its indoor pool and tennis courts.

"Don't worry," said Kaylee. "I'll keep the date open." She looked at the sheet in her hand once more. "Annie said they needed twelve dancers. That means not everyone who applies will get to go to Prairieland."

Caitlin put an arm around her friend's shoulders and grinned conspiratorially. "In case you haven't noticed, you're getting to be a pretty good dancer. You'll get picked for sure!"

Caitlin's faith in her gave Kaylee confidence as she rode home from Paavo with her father. She showed him the handout.

"Prairieland?" her father said, impressed. Then he frowned. "I doubt that we can afford that."

"It doesn't cost anything, Dad," Kaylee said impatiently. "It's a show."

Kaylee had done a couple of shows during the summer. One had been at a nursing home, where most of the residents had seemed only dimly aware that they were not watching the flickering images of some forty-year-old TV program. The other had been at Milwaukee's annual Irish festival in August. That had been shock-and-awe. Trean Gaoth had staged an hour-long, high-energy celebration of Irish dance that kept the crowd of several thousand on their feet and cheering through most of it. *People really go nuts over this stuff, don't they?* her father had observed.

"It'll be like when we performed in August," added Kaylee. "Only indoors."

Her father nodded, handed back the paper. "Sounds great!

It seemed to Kaylee that there was approval in his tone--not as fierce as it would have been if she had told him she had decided to rejoin the Green Storm.

But approval just the same.

Seven

Sunday afternoon, Kaylee sat with her grandmother, hand-sewing the last of her shamrock lap quilt, surrounded by boxes, sewing machines and chairs stacked with cloth and patterns. Grandma Birdsall's wall clock ticked away nestled amidst old framed photographs, an odd thing to hear on Sunday afternoons when the sound of Kaylee's voice normally drowned out such insignificant background noise.

"You're quiet today," observed Grandma Birdsall, casting a sideways glance at her granddaughter.

Kaylee remained silent for a few more moments before replying, and when she did, it was hardly worth hearing. "Just thinking."

Naturally her grandmother could not help but reply to this remark with *About what?* and Kaylee could not help but utter the automatic *Nothing* in response. This led to several more questions from Grandma Birdsall, each of which was rewarded with a one-word answer that did not really answer anything. Finally she said, "Well, if you want to talk, I'm always here for you dear."

"I know. Thanks Grandma."

This was followed by a deeper silence than before.

Finally: "So . . . how's school?"

Kaylee sighed heavily in response.

Grandma glanced toward the window. "Maybe your friend Jackie will bike over again today."

Kaylee kept her eyes down. “I doubt it.” Another long silence followed before Kaylee continued.

“Bet they’re enjoying soccer practice today. Dad and Will.”

Grandma Birdsall now smiled knowingly at her granddaughter. “You miss soccer, don’t you?”

Kaylee squirmed a bit. “Sometimes. But mostly, you know, I miss the time with Dad. The only time we spend together these days is when he’s driving me to or from dance lessons. And Mom does that half the time.”

Grandma Birdsall thought while she worked at the edging of her own quilt, an early-American flag-inspired design with reds, whites and blues. “Why don’t you find something else the two of you can do together.”

“Like what?” asked Kaylee, intrigued.

“Well,” said her grandmother, “what does he like besides soccer?”

“More soccer,” Kaylee said immediately.

“Your father is pretty handy with tools,” said Grandma Birdsall. “Maybe the two of you could build something together.”

Kaylee sighed. “He’s handy. I’m pathetic. In second grade, they sent wood home with us. I worked for three solid days until I built a shoebox.”

“That’s not so bad,” said Grandma Birdsall.

“It was supposed to be a birdhouse!” said Kaylee.

Grandma Birdsall paused in her sewing. “Your father must like something besides soccer.”

“Food,” said Kaylee. “He likes to eat. Pizza, steak, Chinese, Mexican . . . anything.”

“Maybe you could make a special meal for him,” suggested Grandma Birdsall. “Something for just the two of you.”

Now Kaylee nodded. “Yeah. He’d probably like that. I made lasagna once. Mom showed me how. I think I could do that.”

"Splendid!" said Grandma Birdsall. "Why don't we stop for today? It's so nice outside. You'd better enjoy it before the really cold weather gets here!"

Kaylee took her grandmother's advice, giving the old woman a kiss on the cheek as she made her exit. On her way out the door, Kaylee grabbed a light jacket and then stood in the driveway enjoying the combination of cool autumn air and warm sunlight on her face. Of course, it was only moments before her feet started moving in Irish dance steps.

She finished her jig and was halfway through her reel when her father's car pulled up the short driveway. Tom O'Shay and Will got out, chattering about the just finished practice.

"Hey!" called her father, smiling as he spotted Kaylee, who had hopped onto the lawn. Then he and Will resumed their walk to the house and their conversation.

"You're really handling the ball well," she heard her father say to Will. "But you still have to work on passing. That was my specialty when I played. Someday I'll have to get that tape from Buzz so I can show you."

"That tape" came up in conversation every now and then at the O'Shay house. In college, Tom O'Shay's team had won the conference title during his senior year. The college TV studio had broadcast the game to the university community and a few videotapes had been made. One had ended up in the hands of her father's friend and former teammate, Buzz Stewart. Three or four times a year, usually after an especially exciting game or practice, Tom O'Shay would resolve to "get that tape from Buzz" so that he could make his own copy. He never followed through, usually because he would get busy with other family matters and forget. Kaylee sensed the tape represented a meaningful part of her father's life.

An idea popped into her head. Kaylee rushed back inside the house and pulled the Rosemary phone directory out of a drawer in the kitchen.

Eight

Mondays at Four Mile Road Elementary School never failed to be blisteringly awful experiences. By the time they had reached the sixth grade, many had already noticed a change in their body chemistry, which meant that weekends did not fully recharge their batteries. As a result, most students arrived at school on Monday morning grumpy and hoping that some aspect of their learning might require them to put their heads down on their desks for 30-45 minutes. However, this never occurred. What did occur was massive amounts of homework to make up for their massively unproductive weekends.

Despite these dismal realities, two good things did happen in school on Monday. Kaylee spoke with Jackie, and Jackie spoke back without yelling. As most meaningful conversations do in sixth grade, theirs occurred in the cafeteria. Kaylee was allowed to get her hot lunch before reporting to Principal Stone's office for her detention, and somehow the two girls found themselves together in line waiting for their trays of mostly beige-colored food. Their dialogue began with a mutual muttering, part greeting, part grunting. It progressed awkwardly to an apology (Kaylee) for whatever it was she had done wrong, followed by a counter-apology (Jackie) for letting whatever it was that Kaylee had done wrong bother her so much, followed by pledges (Kaylee and Jackie) to try to be more considerate of each other's feelings, followed by much giggling (Kaylee and Jackie again), gossip (mostly

Jackie, but Kaylee a little bit) and one rather inappropriate observation about Angelo Zizzo (just Jackie).

"My father wanted me to take down my Angelo Zizzo posters," said Jackie. "He thinks I'm too obsessed because they cover one whole wall of my room. I pointed out to him that if it were really an obsession, there wouldn't still be three walls empty."

Kaylee laughed and told Jackie about the problem with her own father. "I never do things with him anymore. I came up with a plan for us to do something cool together, but I don't think it's going to work." She explained to Jackie about the tape of her father's college soccer team winning the conference title and how she had been hoping to get her hands on a copy of it. "I had it all worked out. Tuesday nights I don't have dance, my dad doesn't work and there's no soccer practice. I was going to call his old friend and get the tape. Then I was going to fix a special dinner for just the two of us and afterwards we could watch the tape together."

"Zizzers, your dad would love that!" Jackie agreed. "So why aren't you going to do it?"

"When I checked the Rosemary telephone book for *Stewart*, I found twelve names," explained Kaylee. "But none of them was a *Buzz* Stewart."

"You're sure he lives in Rosemary?" asked Jackie? Kaylee nodded. "Then the number might be unlisted. Or maybe 'Buzz' was just a nickname, and he's listed in the phone book under his real name. Would anyone other than your dad know his real name?"

"My mom might," Kaylee replied, and her face brightened a bit at the thought, even though it was still Monday and they were still in school.

"Jackie to the rescue," said her friend, performing an exaggerated bow. "So what are you going to fix for supper to show your dad how much you enjoy spending time with him?"

Kaylee answered confidently as she selected a lunch tray from the pile. "Lasagna. I made it once with my mom's help and it turned out pretty good!"

"I should cook *my* dad a meal," said Jackie. "He deserves it! Now that your dad's not coaching the Green Storm, my poor dad has to deal with Brittany all by himself." She looked across the cafeteria to where Brittany usually sat. "Looks like she's not at lunch today. Probably making out with Michael underneath the bleachers in the gym."

Kaylee pantomimed sticking her finger down her throat. Both girls laughed.

Kaylee felt in a good mood even during her usually boring lunch detention, a mood that lasted for almost two whole minutes after she left the principal's office. Then she arrived at her locker, opened it, and discovered what seemed to be vomit splattered all over her books and folders.

Someone threw up! In my locker! But how could someone throw up in my locked locker?

As these thoughts flashed through her brain, Kaylee noticed a cruddy ooze on the inside of her locker door, running down from the grated opening near the top. That explained how it got inside. Then she noticed the smell. It didn't have the nauseating sewer-stench of partially-digested stomach contents. It smelled more like fresh food. As she leaned closer to the mess, she noticed that it was mashed-up, stirred-up, liquefied essence of the meal being served in the cafeteria. In fact, it looked quite similar to the gunk that Jackie had mixed in her milk carton a few days earlier. This gave her a pretty good idea who had dumped it into her locker—and why she hadn't been at her usual spot in the cafeteria.

Brittany Hall.

Nine

The rollercoaster Monday—which had started badly, gotten better for a bit, and then plunged into a bottomless moon crater—improved once the official school day ended. When a person is in sixth grade, the day always improves a bit once the final bell sounds. This particular school day ended more brightly than usual because she and Jackie were friends again, and because it marked the final lunch detention for dumping slop on Brittany. And since Kaylee had finished her homework during lunch detention, the evening stretched ahead of her to use as she wished.

With this gift of free time, she listened to music, arranged her stuffed animals, and practiced her Irish dance steps over and over and over. However, she also made two telephone calls, figuring that it was okay since a week had technically elapsed since the precise minute she had actually slimed Brittany. The first call was to her mother.

"Stitchin' Kitchen," said Beth O'Shay, speaking into the telephone from her workplace, which often kept her busy until after 8 p.m.

"It's me, Mom!" said Kaylee bouncily. She launched directly into an explanation of her Dad Plan.

"That's sweet, honey," said Mrs. O'Shay. "Mr. Stewart's real name is Bernard."

"Bernard?" said Kaylee, surprised. "How did he go from 'Bernard' to 'Buzz'?"

Mrs. O'Shay chuckled. "You'll have to ask your father. I've got to help some customers now! Love you!"

Since it was Monday, she knew that Will and her father would be at soccer practice until seven. This Saturday would be the last outdoor game of the season for the Bullets.

The second *Stewart* in the Rosemary directory was Bernard. Kaylee placed the call, explained who she was, and in less than a minute "Buzz" was gabbing away as if the two of them were old friends.

"Your father was a heck of a player. I'd be happy to make a copy of that tape and drop it off at your house on Monday."

"Oh, I want this to be a surprise," said Kaylee. They finally agreed that Buzz would put the tape in a brown envelope marked with Kaylee's name and drop it off at Four Mile Road Elementary School on Tuesday.

"That'll be perfect!" Kaylee bubbled. "Thanks so much!"

At Thursday's dance practice, Kaylee turned in her form for the Prairieland Country Club Christmas show. The workout began with stretching exercises done while popular music played. Most of the practice was spent drilling the steps for the hornpipe, the dance they had learned most recently. Then they performed portions of their other routines and eventually put them all together into full dances. Toward the end of practice, Tara, a slim, red-haired instructor in her mid-twenties, sat the girls in a semi-circle.

"This year, many of you will dance in your first feis," Tara began. "Some will start as early as January, which gives you about two months. We want you to remember a few things. First, have fun. That's the most important thing of all. If you're not having fun, you're really missing the whole point of Irish dance. Second, relax. Hundreds of other girls will be stepping onto the stage for their first feis. It's no big deal."

No big deal? thought Kaylee. Dancing in her first feis had been on her mind all summer long. She had hardly been able to sleep the night after her mother had signed her up for the Snowfeis. It might be no big deal for Tara, but it was like Super Bowl Sunday as far as Kaylee was concerned.

Tara continued down her feis checklist. Some of the advice Kaylee already knew. However, there were a few things she had not heard, such as giving her shoes a fresh coat of black polish the night before, and that the judges can even deduct points if your sock falls down an inch.

"You'll be representing Trean Gaoth Academy at every feis," concluded Tara. "Enjoy the experience and always do your best."

Annie arrived at this point and added a brief announcement about the Prairieland Christmas show. "Twenty-one dancers from the beginner groups turned in forms. We only need twelve. Next week, Tara will announce the dancers who have been chosen." She paused for a moment as if considering her words carefully. "If you applied but are not chosen to perform at Prairieland, don't worry. There will be many other shows throughout the year."

Yeah, thought Kaylee, *but not like Prairieland!*

"And please know that it's difficult for your teachers to make these choices, too," continued Annie. "Some of you are very close in ability. And remember: You're all Trean Gaoth teammates! We expect you to be good sports and to be supportive of those who do get this opportunity."

With that, Annie gave the girls a warm smile and then headed back toward her office.

As they packed their shoes away, Kaylee babbled nonstop about Prairieland and her fear that she wouldn't make the cut.

"Would you relax already?" Caitlin sighed, rolling her eyes in a way she normally reserved for her parents. She grabbed Kaylee by the shoulders and spun her in a slow circle. "Look around you! How many dancers do you see that you know are better than you?"

Kaylee lowered her voice to a whisper. "I don't know. Three? Four? Five, counting you."

"Exactly!" said Caitlin. "And you don't even know whether all of those girls applied for Prairieland. Their families might have had other things scheduled for that night. Christmas is a busy time of year."

"But," protested Kaylee, "doesn't Trean Gaoth have two or three other beginner classes? What if the other beginners are way better than us?"

"Doubtful," said Caitlin confidently. "But let's pretend you're right. Since you and I are both about the same ability, that means neither of us will be chosen for Prairieland! Then we can both sit home on the night of the performance and watch *Isle of Green Fire* with a big bucket of popcorn between us and wipe each other's tears!" She pretended to wipe tears from Kaylee's eyes, and Kaylee burst out laughing.

On Sunday, Kaylee hardly stopped chattering about the coming week's events as she sat in her grandmother's room. She did not get a great deal of sewing done, either. She explained in detail her secret Tuesday plan, which involved making lasagna for her father. After enjoying a delicious meal, the two of them would see the near-legendary tape. Of course, the excitement would not end there. On Thursday, Kaylee informed her grandmother, she would find out whether she had been chosen for the Prairieland show.

How could any eleven-year-old be expected to wait?

Grandma Birdsall had heard everything half a dozen times already, but being a good grandmother, she listened patiently. She also noticed how little sewing progress Kaylee was making. "I think that's enough for today, dear," said Grandma Birdsall. "I'm afraid I don't have much energy this afternoon."

The Stitchin' Kitchen closed early on Sundays, and so Kaylee's mother dug out her lasagna recipe and took Kaylee to the grocery store. Mother and daughter worked together to find the ingredients, and then added a loaf of garlic bread and a quart of cookie dough ice cream for dessert. After they returned home, Kaylee found herself filled with so much nervous energy that she practiced her Irish dance steps until bedtime.

Monday was what it always was: unpleasant and unremarkable, except that Kaylee had to serve one final lunch detention. The sixth detention had been handed out when she arrived late to class after her locker was super-slimed by an anonymous culprit named Brittany.

She could hardly wait for Tuesday. She would come home from school and begin preparing the meal immediately. Her father would not arrive until about quarter past five, so she would not have to worry about him asking why she was cooking the food. Because of her mother's work schedule, Tom O'Shay made the meals himself, or Kaylee's mother left a turkey breast or casserole in the crock pot. By the time her father arrived, everything would be set. She could almost hear the praises he would offer to her lasagna. But when she presented the tape, his eyes would grow wide in awe. *How did Kaylee do it? She's so much more clever and thoughtful than Will! I must be the luckiest father in the world!* He might jump around the room like a little kid the way he sometimes did after an exciting finish to a soccer game. Or maybe he would just smile, shake his head and gather her up in a tremendous hug. Perhaps he would fall down on his knees and offer up a prayer, thanking God for giving him a daughter who would be so selfless and loving and asking that, in the future, God might help him to find more ways to spend time with her, instead of almost always with her brother who deserved nothing but a life of torment because of his cereal hogging and general annoying nature.

Tuesday during school, the minute hands on the clocks seemed to have been bolted in place. The only location time seemed to progress at its normal pace was during lunch. Kaylee found herself frequently breaking into Irish dance steps as she walked to classes, partly out of nervousness, partly out of joy.

Then, somehow, the school day ended. After stopping at the school office to pick up the package Mr. Stewart had left and after an unendurably long bus ride home, Kaylee and Will barged into the O'Shay kitchen to find a note from their mother.

Grandma took a fall today. She seems okay, but we're at Dr. Holland's office getting her checked.

Kaylee tore the note off the message pad and handed it to her brother. This news seemed to distract Will significantly, for he completely forgot to have his usual three-cookie after school snack. Instead of going up to his room and playing video games on the television there, he actually sat in the living room and began his homework.

Kaylee hoped her grandmother was not badly hurt. Last spring she had passed out. Now she had taken a fall. Getting old did not seem to be much fun at all. She considered postponing her special dinner, but quickly reconsidered. All the supplies had been purchased already. Her father would be home in a couple of hours, and he would need to be fed. As far as her grandmother was concerned, Kaylee could not do much except wait for her mother to call or bring Grandma Birdsall home. She might as well cook.

Her mother and Grandma Birdsall knew about the tape and the special dinner for her father, but Will had no clue. Not that it mattered. There was no way he could betray the secret at this point. Anyway, after homework he would bound up the stairs to his video games, and after that he probably would not notice a herd of elk in the kitchen.

Going to the upper cupboard just to the left of the sink, she brought out the note card on which her mother had jotted the lasagna recipe. After studying it for a moment, Kaylee removed the ground beef from the refrigerator, unwrapped it and broke the mass into smaller pieces in a frying pan. Using a spatula, she chopped at the chunks as they browned until a beefy crumble covered the bottom of the pan. Then she drained the ground beef and set it aside while she brought out the glass baking dish.

Some people boiled the lasagna noodles in advance, but Kaylee's recipe allowed her to set them into the baking dish dry. They would soften as the lasagna cooked. On top of the noodles she spooned pasta sauce, ricotta and mozzarella cheeses, and some of the ground beef. She repeated this until several layers filled the dish, and then she finished off the lasagna with a final layer of sauce and cheese with a sprinkle of oregano. Over the top of the dish she placed aluminum foil, and then Kaylee popped the meal into the oven.

Later, while the lasagna cooled, she would warm the garlic bread.

Wiping down the countertop, Kaylee pulled up a chair and brought out her homework. Because her thoughts kept returning to Grandma Birdsall, she found it difficult to concentrate on her math. Eventually she found her groove, and before she knew it, the math homework was back in her schoolbag and she had reached the halfway point on her language arts worksheet.

The oven timer buzzed her out of the groove.

Using quilted mitts, Kaylee removed the lasagna from the oven and peeled back the aluminum foil. Her creation smelled delicious and looked equally good.

Dad is going to love this, she thought, unable to keep a broad smile from her face. Then, remembering the tape, she fished inside her school bag where it had been since Buzz had delivered it to her school. NORTHLAND COLLEGE SOCCER – CONFERENCE CHAMPIONSHIP GAME had been written on the sleeve in blue marker, presumably by Buzz. Breathing a satisfied sigh, she placed the tape on the counter next to the cooling lasagna.

The kitchen clock above the sink suggested that Kaylee had better pick up the pace. Her father would be home soon. She quickly slipped the garlic bread into the oven and then grabbed two folding TV trays from the rack in a corner of the living room. She set up the tables in her bedroom, facing the television set on her low dresser. The O'Shay living room contained no TV. When Grandma Birdsall had moved in, it had quickly been established that a TV in the living room would keep her awake, and so it had been moved into the O'Shay parents' bedroom. The older television that had formerly sat in their bedroom now rested in Kaylee's room.

She still needed chairs. Then she and her father would be able to feast on lasagna and garlic bread while watching the soccer video he had been telling them about for years. Kaylee returned to the kitchen and proceeded to the door that opened to the basement stairs. Flicking on the lights, she raced down to find the folding chairs.

The O'Shay basement had gray cinder block walls, a concrete floor, and cobweb-laced wooden ceiling joists under which ductwork, pipes and electrical wires had been fastened. The furnace stood inconveniently at the center of the large space. On Kaylee's side of the furnace rested a few pieces of old furniture, a croquet set, several boxes, an exercise bicycle and the washing machine. On the far side, more boxes, old clothing, Christmas decorations, and a workbench littered with tools were all crammed against the walls.

Almost immediately, Kaylee spotted a card table against which four folding chairs had been propped. As she moved to grab two, she heard the kitchen door bang open and her father's heavy footsteps on the floor. "Shoot!" she said, realizing that time gotten away from her. She hoisted a chair under each arm.

Then came an exclamation from above. She heard her own name called, and then her brother's. Will's lighter footsteps sounded above her head as he ran from the living room. She could hear an excited conversation as she lugged the chairs around the furnace, although the floor muffled almost everything except "Where did this come from?"

He must have found the soccer tape!

For a moment, her spirits sank. However, Kaylee quickly realized that her father discovering the tape really changed nothing. This method of surprising him had apparently worked as well as any other. When she emerged from the basement, he would give her a big hug and they would watch Tom O'Shay during his glory days while eating the great lasagna she had made. Will could slurp all he wanted, because he would be eating his meal alone in the kitchen.

Now she heard more energized conversation and the shuffle of feet, both Will's and her father's. Although the words remained muffled, Kaylee could tell that the find had certainly excited her father as much as she had imagined it might. At the foot of the stairs, she decided to lean one chair against the concrete wall, saving it for a second trip. The folding chairs were not especially heavy, but they were awkward.

As she began her ascent, the cacophony of moving feet seemed to reach a crescendo, and then the slamming of the kitchen door silenced everything. *He went outside*, Kaylee thought. *Maybe he left something in the car.* As if on cue, she heard the distant rumble of a car engine, followed by the lower hum of the vehicle being shifted into gear.

Something was wrong.

Kaylee burst into the kitchen, dropped the folding chair and raced to the front window just in time to see her father's car heading down the street. *This can't be happening*, she thought, trying to sort out the events of the last sixty seconds. *Maybe he forgot something at work.* As she moved back into the kitchen, a heaviness seemed to be growing in the pit of her stomach. Maybe he saw the note about Grandma Birdsall and felt he needed to drive to Dr. Holland's office.

In the kitchen, Kaylee saw that the videotape had disappeared from its spot on the counter. In its place was the note pad, and on it, a message from her father:

Beth—Found the tape! Did Buzz drop it off? Big surprise!!! Will and I headed over to Sam Kizobu's house to watch it! See you when we get home!

Next to the notepad, the lasagna pan rested where she had set it to cool. However, more than half of the lasagna had disappeared. A kitchen knife and the aluminum foil roll lay nearby.

They took the lasagna! Her eyes filled with tears. *They took the lasagna I cooked! And the tape! They took everything!*

As the tears rolled down her freckled cheeks, a piercing buzz made her cry out. The kitchen smoke detector had gone off.

Kaylee's garlic bread was burning.

Ten

Kaylee's mother arrived home at nine, anxious and exhausted. Grandma Birdsall had been admitted to the hospital in Paavo as a precaution. There would be more tests in the morning. For now, Grandma Birdsall was fine.

"How did your dinner go?" asked Kaylee's mother, who had only just looked at Kaylee's face since coming through the kitchen door, and who knew instantly that it had not gone well. After Kaylee explained what had happened, a new energy seemed to fill her mother. When Tom O'Shay arrived home fifteen minutes later, she let loose with both barrels.

With her blankets pulled up around her, Kaylee listened from her bedroom, not intentionally, though Mrs. O'Shay delivered the scolding at a volume that made it impossible to ignore.

"I had no idea," Tom O'Shay repeated meekly. "The poor kid. My poor little girl! Aw, this is just great!"

After Beth O'Shay ran out of steam, Tom O'Shay came to Kaylee's room. However, Kaylee pretended to be asleep.

On Wednesday, Kaylee did not see her father until late in the day. When Kaylee hopped on the bus in the morning, Jackie already knew most of what had happened the previous night.

"When your dad showed up at our house with the tape last night, I knew something was wrong. You'd been talking about showing him that tape forever! I wondered if there had been a change of plans, so I didn't say anything at first. But after they watched it, I asked your dad if it was the tape Kaylee had gotten for him."

"What did he say?" asked Kaylee.

"He said no, that your mother must have done it. Then I asked him if he was sure, and he said pretty sure, because he had found it on the kitchen counter. After that, I told him what you had planned. He left our house almost immediately."

After school, Mrs. O'Shay closed the Stitchin' Kitchen early and drove her two children to the hospital in Paavo. Grandma Birdsall would be staying another night in order for the doctors to analyze her test results. Her grandmother seemed weak but restless from what Kaylee could tell. Still, she offered pleasant smiles to everyone, asked about school and apologized profusely for being such a bother to everybody.

"By the way," asked Grandma Birdsall after Will had narrated an especially brutal episode of playground soccer to her, "how did your special dinner go, Kaylee? I'll bet that lasagna you made was delicious!"

Kaylee told her grandmother what had happened.

"Oh no," said Grandma Birdsall, her voice full of sympathy. "You poor dear!"

"Tom feels terrible about it," said Kaylee's mother.

The fact that her father felt terrible moved Kaylee no closer to forgiving him.

They talked for another fifteen minutes, and then Beth O'Shay kissed her mother on the forehead. "It's a school night and the kids have homework."

"Hopefully they'll let me come home tomorrow afternoon," said Grandma Birdsall, accepting hugs from her grandchildren.

As they walked across the hospital parking lot toward the car, Kaylee asked, "Is Grandma Birdsall going to be okay?"

"I hope so," said her mother, but her voice seemed to waver just a bit. In a more resolute tone she added, "You grandmother is a fighter. Do you think she's going to let this thing beat her?"

Both Will and Kaylee offered an ardent no, but on the ride home, Kaylee wondered why she had asked it as a question instead of saying, "Your grandmother is going to beat this thing."

They found Tom O'Shay setting the table when they arrived. Supper talk focused mostly on Grandma Birdsall and on the Stitchin' Kitchen, which would probably lose money this month because of the time Mrs. O'Shay was taking off because of her mother. "I hate closing the shop during the busy weeks leading up to Christmas," said Mrs. O'Shay. "But there's no way around it."

After supper, Mr. O'Shay came to Kaylee's room, where he discovered her wrinkling her nose above her math book.

"Honey," he began, "I'm really sorry about last night."

Kaylee remained silent and kept her attention on the math homework.

"I had no idea," he continued, undaunted. "I thought your mother made the lasagna and that Grandma must have set it out to cool."

Still Kaylee said nothing, although the pencil marks on her math sheet seemed to be getting deeper and darker.

"And when I saw the tape, well, I'd told Mr. Kizoku about it, and I knew Will wanted to see it. We just grabbed a couple pieces of the lasagna and took off."

Kaylee slapped her pencil against the page. "You took half the pan!"

Her reply seemed to startle Mr. O'Shay, but a subtle relaxation of his features suggested he was relieved to have her talking—even angrily.

"All right," he admitted. "I guess we should have slowed down, tried to find out who was home. I'm just a big kid sometimes when it comes to soccer."

Kaylee seemed about ready to throw the pencil at him, when her face suddenly collapsed into a teary mask. Mr. O'Shay knelt next to her and hugged her to his chest.

"I . . . I just wanted it to be you and me," Kaylee sobbed.

"I know sweetheart." Mr. O'Shay stroked his daughter's coppery hair with a hand. "I'm sorry"

"I wanted us to do something together," she continued, her head against his shoulder. "You're always doing things with Will."

Mr. O'Shay sighed. "I know it's been tough on you. And on me, too. I really enjoyed coaching you, kiddo. And you were just starting to really come around as a soccer player. I was so proud of you!"

She pulled away slightly so that she could see her father's face. And he could see her wet cheeks. "You can still be proud of me."

Mr. O'Shay kissed his daughter's forehead. "I am, honey. And don't you worry. I'll find a way to make this up to you! I agree with you. We should spend more time together!"

The following day, Kaylee hardly even minded getting up for school. Thursdays always seemed a little brighter than the rest of the days of the week because of dance class. However, she looked forward to this particular Thursday more than usual. The week had been a disaster up to this point. Her grandmother had been hospitalized, her dinner plans for Tuesday had fallen apart, and she had been depressed all through the school day on Wednesday.

Now, the week's evil magic seemed to be fading. The talk with her father on Wednesday evening had broken the spell. On top of that, her mother had informed her that Grandma Birdsall would be coming home on Thursday afternoon. And, of course, there was dance practice.

But Kaylee knew that dancer selections for the Prairieland Christmas performance dominated her thoughts. In a phone conversation a few days earlier, Caitlin had tried to reassure her friend.

"We're both going to be eating caviar this Christmas," Caitlin had said, and then both girls had laughed. "Face it, Kaylee. You're getting good. You practice all the time, and it shows! Some of the girls in our class never fall off the couch between Thursdays!"

Both girls spent an unusual amount of time giggling during the Thursday practice. Yet, both were as sharp as they had ever been when it came to their dancing.

"I wish the first feis was this weekend!" said Caitlin at break time, chugging a quarter of her water bottle. "I'm so ready!"

At the end of practice, Tara and Miss Helen gathered all the girls at the edge of the dance floor and complimented them on their efforts. Then Tara spoke about Prairieland, and Kaylee clenched her fists.

"Thank you to everyone who applied. Those who have been chosen will need to attend an extra practice each week on Sunday afternoon. Remember, this is an important show. The people who'll be watching you dance are used to the best of everything!"

Can't she hurry up? Kaylee thought to herself. *I'll explode if I have to wait much longer!*

"The list of dancers for Prairieland is on the bulletin board near the front door," announced Tara. "If you or your parents have any questions, have them call or e-mail me."

Caitlin and Kaylee had never changed into their street shoes so quickly. Kaylee's father arrived at the edge of the dance floor only to see his smiling daughter wave and race past him, heading back in the direction he had just come.

Several other girls pressed close to the sheet pinned onto the board. Kaylee decided to wait patiently, but that idea flew out the window when Caitlin shouted, "Hurry up!" to the girls in front. Most of the girls came away beaming, though Kaylee did notice one whose cheeks were red with disappointment.

"I see my name!" said Caitlin in a front-row-at-a-rock-concert voice. "Cinderella is going to the ball!"

"What about me?" asked Kaylee, pushing to the front. "Did you see me?"

Caitlin looked. She frowned. Then the delight drained from her face. Kaylee's eyes raced up and down the page.

"I'm not there. I didn't make it."

"Oh . . ." Caitlin's voice trailed off.

"Hey sweetheart," said Mr. O'Shay, coming up behind Kaylee. "What's up? You look a little sad."

Now Caitlin spoke angrily, though she kept her voice low so that it could not be heard back at the dance floor. "This is so not fair! You are better than at least half the girls on that list!"

Mr. O'Shay squinted at the bulletin board. "Is it about the Prairieland performance? Oh, honey, I'm sorry!"

"I don't even feel like going anymore!" said Caitlin, crossing her arms defiantly in front of herself.

"No," said Kaylee, trying to hold her voice steady. "You've got to go. It's a big honor. They had to make cuts somewhere."

"But you're better than that!" protested Caitlin. "You should go right now and ask Tara why she didn't choose you!"

Mr. O'Shay brushed his hand across his daughter's cheek. "Did you want me to talk to Tara?"

Kaylee shook her head. "I'll do it."

Normally she was not brave enough to question the wisdom of an adult. If she felt that a teacher had misjudged one of her assignments in school, she usually just shrugged and accepted her fate. If old Mr. Nichols who lived down the street yelled at her, accusing her of riding her bicycle across his lawn, she apologized even though she knew she hadn't done it.

But this was Irish dance.

"Maybe there's some dance step I'm not doing right." Kaylee lifted her chin, sniffed slightly as she spoke to Caitlin and her father. "If I find out now, then maybe I can fix it before my first feis in February."

Kaylee walked back toward the dance floor. The next class had just begun their stretching. Tara and Miss Helen stood watching along the side. When Kaylee asked Tara if she had a moment, Tara excused herself and walked back towards the offices with Kaylee, stopping in front of one.

"I know you're busy," said Kaylee awkwardly, afraid she might cry at any moment. "But you said to talk to you if we had any questions about the Prairieland list."

Tara looked directly at Kaylee, unblinking. "You want to know why your name isn't on the list?"

Kaylee nodded. "I think I'm doing okay. I'm really improving, I know that."

Tara nodded. "You're getting to be a good dancer."

"But," said Kaylee, her eyes drifting toward the floor, "not good enough?"

Tara sighed. "I know this is hard. Prairieland is an important show. It's a big commitment."

"I guess," said Kaylee softly, though she did not really understand what this had to do with her name not being on the list.

"Let me," said a husky voice. Miss Helen stood behind Tara, and motioned for her to supervise the class. Miss Helen towered over Kaylee and wore an expression that was stern yet sympathetic.

"I made the decision to leave you off the list," said Miss Helen. Kaylee started to reply, but Miss Helen held a finger to her lips. "Kaylee, you're probably one of the two or three best dancers in your class. You must know that."

This brought Kaylee's head up. It sounded like a compliment, if she had heard it correctly. Why, then, had Miss Helen omitted her name? Her teacher continued.

"Even so, I'm still not sure about you. I'm not sure you can make the big commitment."

"I practice all the time," said Kaylee, a slight pleading tone in her voice. "You can ask my dad. Every day!"

"So did Lizzie Martin," said Miss Helen.

Now Kaylee understood.

They had all heard the story. Lizzie Martin had been Miss Helen's best dancer sixteen years ago, probably good enough to place at the World Championships. Miss Helen had poured her heart into training her to be the best. But Lizzie had quit Irish dance in favor of soccer. Miss Helen was still bitter over the incident.

Then last spring, Kaylee had chosen a soccer tournament over Trean Gaoth's St. Patrick's Day performance. Annie had been fine about it, realizing that there would be many other Irish dance opportunities, but that it would be Kaylee's last soccer tournament with her father as coach. Miss Helen, however, had seen it differently.

"Many of the girls at Trean Gaoth are ready to make dance their top priority," said Miss Helen. "Maybe you're ready to do that, too. But until I see evidence of that, I have to reward the girls who have already shown me that Irish dance is their passion." She bent her head to try and make eye contact with Kaylee, whose face had tilted toward the floor once again. "It's not the end of the world. You've only been dancing a year. If you're dedicated, good things will happen in their time."

Kaylee shuffled back to where her father stood waiting next to the bulletin board. Caitlin's mother had apparently already whisked her away. "What did she say?" asked Mr. O'Shay as he opened the door and escorted his daughter out into the darkened parking lot.

She thought about the St. Patrick's Day soccer tournament last spring, about how well she had played, and about how proud her father had been.

The last game with her father as her coach.

Kaylee offered a weak smile as they climbed into the car. "She said I need more practice."

Eleven

For awhile, Kaylee had dreaded the rapidly approaching Christmas vacation. This, of course, was completely insane, for it marked the first time in her life—perhaps the first time in any child's life—that she had not eagerly, ravenously, gleefully charted the exact seconds until the freedom bell on December's last school day sounded. However, December brought with it the Prairieland Christmas show, which would not include Kaylee.

It also brought a two-week intermission between dance classes. Miss Helen's decision to snub her for the Christmas show had motivated Kaylee to work even harder. She knew that she could not sit around doing nothing except eating Christmas cookies all vacation long. She had to dance every day to stay in top shape.

"You sure are dedicated," said Mrs. O'Shay, watching her daughter practice in her bedroom one afternoon a few days after Christmas. "Do all the girls at Trean Gaoth practice as much as you do?"

Kaylee smiled proudly. "I know Caitlin practices a lot."

Mrs. O'Shay shook her head incredulously, and then stepped into the bedroom to give her daughter a hug. "You're a good dancer, honey. I'll bet as good as anyone in your class."

"Thanks Mom," said Kaylee, returning the hug. Although her mother had not actually mentioned that Kaylee should have been chosen for the Prairieland

Christmas show, Kaylee figured that was the unspoken message.

The following day, Caitlin called. They buzzed for more than an hour, discussing what each girl had gotten for Christmas. Kaylee's favorite present was a navy-blue dress bag with the Trean Gaoth logo—a dove rising above a stylized gust of wind, surrounded by a wreath of Celtic knot. Caitlin's was a laptop. Eventually the conversation tiptoed into the subject of the Prairieland show.

"You can be honest with me," said Kaylee. "It was great, wasn't it?"

Caitlin, who at first had attempted to downplay the event, could not hold back after receiving such an invitation. "It was awesome," she gushed. "That place is like a palace inside a castle inside a mansion!" She painted the whole picture for Kaylee: all the guests in formal attire, a chandelier that looked like it belonged in Phantom of the Opera, gold faucets in the restrooms. "And they served those little hot dogs I love in that spicy sauce!" added Caitlin.

Apparently Trean Gaoth had been a hit with the party guests, too. "They all seemed fascinated by our wigs," said Caitlin, and Kaylee could tell from the tone of her voice that her friend was probably performing a major eye roll. "'Is that your own hair?' I don't know how many times I heard that!"

Kaylee smiled wanly. "Wish I could have seen the show. The little hot dogs. And everything."

After a pause, Caitlin replied, "Yeah. If you'd been there, the night would have been perfect. That was really rotten what Miss Helen did."

"No biggie," Kaylee said, but her jaw tightened as she did so. Inside, she felt hurt, cheated and angry.

"Hey!" said Caitlin suddenly. "Are we going to do a sleepover again this year?"

The previous year, Caitlin had invited Kaylee and two other girls from their Trean Gaoth class to stay overnight at her house in Paavo.

"Sounds great!" said Kaylee.

"Maybe we could do it at your house this year," suggested Caitlin.

The idea caught Kaylee by surprise. Her house was nowhere near as big or as nice as Caitlin's. Kaylee's ghillies and hard shoes were secondhand. Her grandmother had sewn her school dress. Sometimes the world of Irish dance—where everything seemed so expensive—felt alien to her, a world that she might visit for awhile, but where she could not remain for long. What would Caitlin and the other girls think when they arrived at her little home that barely had enough room for two very small children and a grandmother?

"I'll have to ask my mom," said Kaylee.

After she hung up, Kaylee felt confused and cornered. She always had a great time with Caitlin and the other girls, but she was not anxious to have them visit her ordinary little house. She could easily tell Caitlin that her mother had said no to the sleepover request. In the end, though, lying to Caitlin was useless. Caitlin's mother frequently talked with Beth O'Shay, either by phone or at the Stitchin' Kitchen. Mrs. Hubbard would surely ask about the sleepover, and if Kaylee's mom appeared clueless, Caitlin would become suspicious.

In fact, Kaylee did not have to ponder the problem for long. Her mother brought up the subject the following evening at supper.

"Mrs. Hubbard called today," Beth O'Shay began. "She says you girls are planning a sleepover. Maybe at our house this year."

Kaylee's face reddened slightly. "Oh yeah. I was going to talk to you about that."

"I think it's a great idea!" said her mother, who seemed almost as excited as if she were one of the eleven-year-old girls involved.

"But," argued Kaylee weakly, stirring green beans with a fork, "where will we all sleep?"

Mrs. O'Shay frowned over the coffee cup held beneath her chin, as if the answer were so obvious that Kaylee should have twisted an ankle upon it by this time. "Well, there's your bed. And there should be space for three sleeping bags on your floor."

"But what if I want to sleep on the floor, too?" asked Kaylee.

"Oh, I'm sure you can fit," said her father. "Sleeping bags don't take up much room."

Kaylee nodded. Her brother slurped his food. Meat loaf. *How could anyone slurp meat loaf?* Kaylee wondered, annoyed. *I'll bet this kid could slurp a brick!*

"They'll want pizza," said Kaylee suddenly. "Getting that much pizza delivered is going to be awfully expensive."

"We can make our own pizza," said Mrs. O'Shay, smiling. "I have a great crust recipe. And we'll cut up fresh mushrooms and onions and peppers. It'll be more fun than ordering from some pizza place." Then her mother's eyes took on the concerned sort of look they often got when someone had a fever or sore throat. "Kaylee, you almost sound like you don't want to have a sleepover. Is everything okay? Did you and Caitlin have a fight?"

"Everything's fine," said Kaylee curtly, and she felt the warmth in her cheeks again. "I really do want a sleepover. It's just . . ."

Mrs. O'Shay waited. "Just?"

Kaylee's mind raced. She had to say something, but not *Our house is too small, we don't have a big-screen TV, delivered pizza tastes ten times better, and everything we own is either secondhand or nearly worn-out.*

"I just wish," she continued, grateful for sudden inspiration, "that we had some decent movies. Girls like to watch movies all night long at sleepovers."

"You could show 'em my soccer tape," her father said brightly. Then he raised both palms and grinned sheepishly. "Sorry. Joke. Joke. I know that's still a sensitive subject."

"What about your *Isle of Green Fire* DVD?" asked Mrs. O'Shay.

"Mom, these are Irish dancers," said Kaylee, tapping the end of her fork on the tabletop. "They've all seen it a bazillion times."

"If they like it that much," said Will, his mouth half full of meat, "they won't mind seeing it a bazillion and one."

"I know," said Mrs. O'Shay suddenly. "I can check out some videos from the public library. It's free. Kaylee, you can come with me a day or two before to help pick them out."

"From the library?" Kaylee looked at her family as if they had been replaced by space aliens. "They're not going to want to watch 'Molecules in Action' or something they might see in science class."

"You can check out popular movies from the library, too," noted Mrs. O'Shay. "The same ones they have at the video store. Trust me, Kaylee."

So it was settled, thought Kaylee. Four sleeping bags in a sardine can, do-it-yourself pizza, and library videos on an eighteen-inch TV. Whoopee.

Later that evening, Kaylee's father visited her in her room, where she was doing what she always did when she felt gloomy or anxious: watching *Isle of Green Fire*. "Hey, kiddo," he said as he sat beside her on the bed. "You haven't seemed quite yourself this Christmas vacation, and I think I know what's going on."

"You do?" said Kaylee uneasily, putting the DVD on pause.

"You're still upset about what happened," he said. "The lasagna dinner. I don't blame you, honey, and you know how sorry I am."

Kaylee breathed a subtle sigh of relief. "I'm all right, Dad. Really."

Tom O'Shay smiled. "You're a great kid, Kaylee. But even if you're okay with it, it still bothers me that I messed up your plans. I know how special you wanted that evening to be. So I've been thinking of some way to make it up to you ever since."

"You really don't have to do that, Dad."

Her father's eyes dropped to the floor. "I know. But I enjoyed those times when we worked together. Me as coach, you as the coachee."

Kaylee smiled.

"Well, Jackie's father just informed me of an opportunity," he continued. "The first Sunday in January, Mr. Beck is going to be out of town. He's the assistant coach of the Green Storm during the indoor season. His daughter will be gone, too, and maybe a couple of other girls. In fact, it looks like we might not have the minimum number of players. That means we'd have to forfeit the game."

Kaylee nodded, wondering where this was going.

"Unless," continued Mr. O'Shay, "we can find another player."

Kaylee's head popped up as she suddenly understood. "You want *me* to play?"

"Only if you want to," said her father. "Mr. Kizobu asked me to help coach the team for that game, and I just thought it might be an opportunity for us to do something together again."

Kaylee did not know what to say.

"It'd just be for that one game," noted her father. "If you don't want to, we can probably find someone else.

And you and I could go to a movie or bowling some other time. So no pressure. The opportunity is there if you want."

It was true that she missed playing soccer for her father. And it was only for one game, so there wouldn't be a conflict with dance.

How could she say no?

Twelve

Kaylee had worried that her friends might laugh at her tiny house. It did not have high ceilings like many of the rooms in Caitlin's house. The O'Shay white, Cape Cod-style house nestled in a neighborhood where most of the modest homes seemed to need new paint. The girls had slept in Caitlin's basement at last year's holiday sleepover, but Caitlin's basement had been carpeted and furnished as nicely as the upstairs. If they slept in Kaylee's basement, they would be sleeping on bare, concrete floors.

As it turned out, Kaylee had no reason to worry. No one said a thing. In fact, the girls seemed not to care whether they were sleeping in a house or a hollow log. All that really mattered was that they were together, large quantities of pizza would be consumed, and they would stay up most of the night.

"You have a charming house!" Mrs. Hubbard said graciously as she dropped off Caitlin, Meghan and April, all of whom lived in Paavo.

Kaylee's mom offered a wary smile. "I hope it's still charming by tomorrow."

Mrs. Hubbard laughed. "The girls were wonderful last year. They tried really hard to stay awake all night, but I didn't hear much after midnight."

Mrs. O'Shay's only real worry was that the silliness in Kaylee's room might keep her mother awake. As a result, the O'Shay parents would be sleeping in Grandma Birdsall's room across from Kaylee's. Kaylee's mother had moved Grandma into her parents' room for the night so that the girls would be less likely to keep her awake with their late night chatter.

"She needs her sleep," said Mrs. O'Shay. "She's on new medication and she gets very tired."

After Mrs. Hubbard left, the girls rolled out their sleeping bags, which completely covered the floor. "This is sweet," said April. "We can all share the tortilla chips at the same time!"

"And Kaylee's got a TV!" said Meghan, pointing. "We can watch movies all night long!"

When Kaylee's father heard this, his face fell. "Maybe *I'll* sleep in the basement tonight," he said to Mrs. O'Shay.

I guess it doesn't matter whether we've got a big house, Kaylee thought as she watched her friends giggle and throw chips at each other. For awhile, she had wondered whether her family really fit in with Irish dancing. After all, everything seemed so expensive.

The shoes cost a fortune, but they had found secondhand ghillies and hard shoes.

The lessons and school dress were expensive, but her grandmother had helped with those.

Her house was tiny, but it seemed like her friends wouldn't have cared if she lived in a cave.

Maybe the O'Shays fit in after all.

*

A few days later, Mr. Kizobu gathered the Green Storm team at the Four Mile Road Elementary School gymnasium, and it was almost like Kaylee had never been gone. Not only did she blend in with the group on the field, but Brittany resumed her insults: "Hustle, O'Shrimp! Did you get shorter *and* slower during the past year?"

Yes, it was just like old times.

It felt good to wear the green jersey again. It felt good to run. It especially felt good to see her father on the sideline, clapping his hands and offering encouragement when she did something well.

It felt good to see Jackie smile, too.

However, when Kaylee spoke to Caitlin on the telephone later, she could tell that her friend from dance class was not smiling. "You'd better not let Miss Helen know you're playing soccer again," cautioned Caitlin. "She already thinks you're nearly as wicked as Lizzie Martin."

"It's one game," replied Kaylee. "Relax."

Besides, there was no rule against playing soccer. You could do anything you wanted when you weren't at dance practices, shows or competitions. Soccer, softball, sumo wrestling, you name it. Kaylee figured Miss Helen was just overly sensitive because she'd been burned by this Lizzie chick.

Although Caitlin was not satisfied with Kaylee's response, she was too excited to talk about soccer for very long. The Chicago Winter Arts Feis was coming up on Saturday.

"It's the very first feis of the new year!" Caitlin said excitedly.

Kaylee's mother had given her permission to go along with the Hubbards. Kaylee's first feis, the Milwaukee Snowfeis, would not be until mid-February. "We can't afford to sign you up for every feis," her mother had said. "The feis in Milwaukee is nearby. We'll start with that one."

At first, Kaylee pouted. Her mother, however, convinced her that there might be advantages to waiting. "You can go along with Caitlin and see how a feis works. Then you won't feel so intimidated when you compete in your first one." Although Kaylee agreed so that there would not be an argument, she pointed out to her mother that Caitlin hardly seemed to feel intimidated.

On Saturday morning, Kaylee's alarm went off at 5:30. The Hubbards arrived at six to take her to the feis.

Mrs. O'Shay, dressed in a frayed terrycloth robe, unleashed an enormous yawn and then wrapped a hug around her daughter. "Have a good time, sweetheart." She gave Kaylee a brown paper bag containing a couple of oat bars and a peanut butter sandwich. "You'll have to tell me all about it tonight."

The ride to Chicago in the Hubbard minivan took a little more than two hours, though it seemed to Kaylee that they were going through toll booths about every five minutes after they crossed the border into Illinois. Mr. Hubbard, a tall man in a striped pullover sweater, drove the van. He smiled often, and his moustache seemed to dance whenever this happened. It was the first time Kaylee had met Caitlin's father, whose job during the week had something to do with investments—whatever that was. Mrs. Hubbard sipped coffee in the front passenger seat and the two girls chatted excitedly in the back.

After exiting the tollway and twisting around several corners, Mr. Hubbard parked in a ramp near the lakefront and they walked to the hotel where the feis was being held. Parents and young girls with dress bags converged on the main entrance from all directions. The front of the hotel had been constructed of dark, polished marble with gold metal trim. "It looks like a palace!" said Caitlin.

"Are you nervous?" asked Mr. Hubbard, beaming down at his daughter.

"A little," said Caitlin. "But I know I'm going to do great!"

"That's the spirit!" said Mr. Hubbard brightly. "But what makes you so confident?"

"Well," said Caitlin as they made their way through the revolving front door. "Look who's here to give me support? My mom, my dad . . . and my best friend!"

When Kaylee heard that, she knew that both of them would have a great day.

Thirteen

Kaylee's friend carried her own dress bag across the hotel lobby, but Mr. Hubbard was loaded down with all kinds of bundles so that he looked like a pack mule. They followed signs to a hallway leading to conference and meeting rooms set up for the registration and dancing. After a wait in line that Mr. Hubbard described as "not too bad" and which Mrs. Hubbard said took "forever", Caitlin emerged with her competitor number. Then Mrs. Hubbard checked a card, consulted a map, and they headed farther down the hall.

"The card says most of Caitlin's dances will be on stage seven," said Mrs. Hubbard over her shoulder. They weaved through a thickening crowd, rounded a corner and arrived at a meeting room with a number seven on an easel near the door.

The carpeted room was at least four times as big as one of the classrooms at Four Mile Road Elementary School. At the far end was the stage, a plywood platform twenty or thirty feet across, built on a framework of two-by-fours. Next to it was another easel, supporting a sheet filled with numbers and letters that seemed to have no meaning at all. A table sat in front of the stage with a single chair tucked behind it. A triple row of folding chairs lined the left side of the stage, but no one sat in these. Half a dozen additional rows of folding chairs fanned out in front of the stage, and these were beginning to fill. Instead of heading for the chairs, Mrs. Hubbard went to the back of the room where Kaylee noticed a handful of families had spread out blankets and set up folding chairs as if readying themselves for a picnic.

"April has an older sister who has been dancing in feisanna for several years," explained Mrs. Hubbard as her husband spread out a blanket of his own. "Her mother told me we should find a spot at the back of the room early and set up 'camp'." Now Caitlin's father set up the folding chairs he had been carrying and Caitlin slung her dance bag over one of them.

"Dancing begins at nine," said Mrs. Hubbard. Glancing at her wristwatch. "We'd better start getting you ready." As she quickly pulled Caitlin's makeup pouch out of her dress bag, the pouch slipped out of her hands and several round makeup containers rolled onto the floor. Flustered, Mrs. Hubbard hurried to retrieve them.

Another mother whose blanket had been rolled out next to Camp Hubbard, knelt and picked up one of the containers. "Looks like no damage done," she said cheerily, handing it back to Mrs. Hubbard. She glanced at Caitlin. "First feis?"

Mrs. Hubbard thanked the woman and nodded.

"This is our third year," said the woman, pointing to her daughter who was seated in a folding chair in the middle of the blanket, reading a book. She introduced herself as Addy Burrows and her daughter Dayna. Both mother and daughter were painfully thin with short, straight, blonde hair. Dayna seemed relaxed in a dark green top and bundies and appeared in no rush to get ready.

"There's really no need to hurry," said Mrs. Burrows.

Mrs. Hubbard opened the booklet that showed the stages and the order of dances. "Caitlin's in the third dance on this stage," she said, pointing to the top of a long column of numbers.

"Dayna's a little after that," said Mrs. Burrows. "But these competitions hardly ever start on time. After you've done a few, you'll see."

Caitlin's mother thanked Mrs. Burrows, but the advice did not seem to convince her. "You never know," Mrs. Hubbard said warily to her daughter. "Since it's your first feis, I'd rather not take any chances."

Caitlin had been wearing pajama pants and a Trean Gaoth Dance Academy sweatshirt. Now she pulled off the sweatshirt to reveal a shiny blue short-sleeved top. Kaylee had one like it, made of a special material that was supposed to help keep the sweat off your dance dress. After her mother had signed her up for the Milwaukee Snowfeis, she had wondered whether she would feel embarrassed if she had to change into her dress in a room like this where anybody could look right at you and see your shiny, blue underwear. As she looked around, however, she saw lots of girls sitting around in shorts and t-shirts and outfits that looked dangerously close to underwear. No one seemed the least bit concerned. *I guess it's like joggers,* Kaylee thought. *They wear underwear-sized outfits right down the middle of the road!*

Mrs. Hubbard began the process of pinning up Caitlin's hair. Then the wig came out of its box. Although a few schools did not require the tightly curled hair, the vast majority of dancers—including Kaylee—wore a special curly dance wig that was matched precisely to the color of their hair. While Mrs. Hubbard inserted the hairpins, Caitlin glued her poodle socks in place, and laced on her ghillies. Finally she slipped into her school dress, and Kaylee helped lace the cape onto the back.

Standing back to inspect her friend, Kaylee jabbed a thumb into the air. "You look awesome!"

"Why don't you run over to the stage and warm up a bit," suggested Mrs. Hubbard.

Caitlin nodded and Kaylee followed her through the swirling human sea.

Several other dancers were trying out the stage, including a couple of boys that looked to be about Kaylee's age. Caitlin danced a bit, watched a few of the other girls, danced a bit more and then headed back toward the rear of the room.

"I'm so nervous I'll probably forget all my steps," said Caitlin.

"We'll never forget," laughed Kaylee. "The way Tara and Miss Helen drill them into us they're permanently burned into our brains."

When they arrived at their camp, Mrs. Hubbard carefully examined her daughter to see that nothing had been smudged, wrinkled or bumped out of place during the warm-up. Then she rechecked her watch. "Five after nine," she muttered, and simultaneously snuck a guilty look in the direction of the Burrows blanket. Mrs. Burrows seemed interested in a book of her own, and Dayna appeared no more anxious to prepare than before.

"Well," said Mr. Hubbard, slapping his knees as he rose off his chair, "I'm going to see if I can find something to eat. Want anything, dear?"

"I'll eat later," said his wife anxiously.

Caitlin began to place her order. "See if they've got bagels and—"

Mrs. Hubbard cut her off. "Not before your first dance. You could be up any minute now, and you don't want to feel sick to your stomach. We'll get something when there's a little break."

Caitlin sighed and slumped back in her chair.

"What about you, Miss O'Shay?" asked Mr. Hubbard. "Care to join me?"

Kaylee had to admit that she was starved, and so she gladly accepted Mr. Hubbard's invitation. She had brought along a few dollars from her weed pulling money just in case she found something a bit more exciting than oat bars.

"Arthur," Mrs. Hubbard said in a worried tone, "you'll miss your daughter's first dance ever in competition!"

"Oh, he's got plenty of time," said Mrs. Burrows casually, who had apparently caught their conversation and was now looking at them over the top of her book. "You can see that there's no judge at the table." Glancing toward the stage, Kaylee could see that this was true. "And they haven't even done the anthems yet."

"Anthems?" This came from Mr. Hubbard.

"Someone usually sings or plays the national anthems to officially start a feis," explained Mrs. Burrows. "The Star-spangled Banner, the Irish national anthem, and O Canada!"

"Canada?" said Caitlin. "Why Canada?"

"Irish dance is big in Canada," said Mrs. Burrows, "and lots of Canadian girls travel to Chicago and other U.S. cities to compete."

"But," sputtered Mrs. Hubbard, glancing yet again at her watch, "it's quarter past nine! Shouldn't they have done that by now?"

Mrs. Burrows smiled kindly. "Like I said, these competitions hardly ever start on time."

"We'll hurry," promised Mr. Hubbard, patting his wife on the back, and then he and Kaylee began weaving through the crowd.

Outside of room number seven, the crowd seemed even thicker. There were parents, girls of all ages in dresses or sweats, and a few boys in dark pants boiling through the wide corridor. Kaylee passed other rooms with large placards outside advertising STAGE SIX, STAGE FIVE and so forth. She glanced inside one room quickly and found dozens of girls camped out at the back, just like in their room.

I never knew there were this many Irish dancers in the whole world! thought Kaylee.

After a short distance they emerged into an immense reception area. On the left were vendors selling Irish clothing, jewelry, t-shirts, knick-knacks, even sections of dance floor. On the right were tables containing trophies and boxes of what appeared to be medals. A little farther down the room was a roped off area with large charts on the wall. The numbers on the charts seemed similar to the numbers Kaylee had seen on the easel next to stage seven.

"This must be where the results get posted after each dance," said Mr. Hubbard. He did not slow down, but rather increased his pace as he spied his destination ahead: the food.

Twenty or thirty tables stood at the far end of the room, flanked by two long counters with menus hanging above them. Only a few people waited in the lines now, but Kaylee guessed it would get very busy near lunch time when the thousands of girls, boys and parents grew hungry.

Mr. Hubbard ordered coffee and two doughnuts for himself as well as bagels to take back to his wife and Caitlin. Kaylee chose a blueberry bagel for herself, which Mr. Hubbard paid for even though she had her money out of her pocket.

"Thanks," she said, hungrily, tearing into the bagel.

As they turned to head back to stage seven, a woman's voice boomed over the public address system, welcoming competitors and spectators to the Winter Arts Feis, and then inviting everyone to stand for the Irish National Anthem. Since they did not know the words, Kaylee and Mr. Hubbard paused and nibbled respectfully as the music played, and then nibbled some more during the Canadian National Anthem. However, they sang the Star-Spangled Banner.

They found Mrs. Hubbard fussing over Caitlin when they returned to the camp—probably for the zillionth time. Kaylee noticed that Dayna Burrow had begun to put on her makeup.

"I was starting to get worried," said Mrs. Hubbard. "It's after nine-thirty and I thought you'd miss it."

"Looks like we made it in the nick of time," said Mr. Hubbard popping the last of doughnut number two into his mouth. He winked at Kaylee.

Fifteen minutes later, when the dancing had still not started, Kaylee was certain that the nervous energy trapped inside of Caitlin's mother was going to cause an explosion. "Why is it taking so long? They've already sung the anthems!"

Again, Mrs. Burrows had the answer. "Some of the stages have team dances. Usually all the team dances finish before the individual dances start."

They waited. Caitlin and her mother fussed over whether Caitlin should take off her dress. Just before World War Three seemed ready to break out, the judge—an older, white-haired man in a plaid jacket—arrived at the table, which seemed to give everyone hope. An accordion player, Kaylee noticed, sat at one corner.

It took another five minutes for the judge to finish shuffling the papers in front of him. Two young women then motioned to the row of dancers that had been sitting in the front row along the side. Twenty-two young girls rose in unison and walked to the back of the stage where they formed a line facing the judge. Kaylee noticed they all wore numbers on the front which looked to be fastened around their waists by yarn or ribbon. They stood, some smiling, some stone-faced, a couple fidgeting anxiously while the judge seemed to be checking the numbers against a sheet of paper on the table in front of him.

Mr. Hubbard leaned toward Kaylee and whispered. "I think we've got time to go back for more doughnuts and bagels if you want."

Kaylee laughed.

"What did you say, dear?" Mrs. Hubbard asked her husband.

"Just commenting on how colorful all the costumes are," said Mr. Hubbard, smiling.

He was right, Kaylee noticed. The costumes seemed to represent every color in the rainbow. There was even one Trean Gaoth school dress in the group, though Kaylee did not recognize the girl.

There were also three girls wearing the white Golden Academy school dress.

"They think they're so good," whispered Caitlin. "I hear they're not even allowed to talk to girls from other dance schools when they're at a feis."

At a sign from the judge, familiar music began to play, and something happened that Kaylee had not anticipated: She suddenly felt nervous, almost as if *she* would have to dance in front of all these people.

The first two girls on the left stepped to center stage, pointed their toes at the appropriate time, and then began their reel. Since the dancers were from a variety of schools, their steps were different even though they danced to the same music. As they neared the end of their dance, the next two stepped out behind them and pointed. The first two came to a stop and bowed, first to the judge and then to the accordionist, as the next two began dancing. This pattern continued until all twenty-two had finished. The crowd applauded their efforts and the first group filed offstage to make room for the next.

"Wow," said Kaylee. "How does the judge ever decide who is best? They all looked good to me!"

"I have no idea," said Mr. Hubbard with a perplexed look.

"His eyes must be able to spot every little mistake," said Caitlin. "Hawks and eagles can spot little mice on the ground from hundreds of feet in the air. A judge's eyes must be like that!"

"Let me straighten your number," Mrs. Hubbard said to her daughter.

Finally Caitlin's turn came. She checked in with the young woman who seemed to be shepherding the dancers onto the stage. Then she sat in a chair with the other girls in her group until it was their turn. As Caitlin in her navy and gold Trean Gaoth dress stood smiling in line facing the judge, Kaylee felt almost as if she were standing there herself. The music began and the first two dancers stepped to the front. Then two more. Then another two. Finally Caitlin and a taller girl in an orange and white dress moved into position, pointed their toes and glided into action. As her friend danced, Kaylee was so excited that her own feet stepped right along with her.

Caitlin moved even more gracefully than in practice, moving first to the front right corner of the stage, then the middle, then the left. Her toes pointed elegantly as she moved in perfect time to the music. The girl in orange was graceful, too, and her steps took her sometimes in a different direction than Caitlin and sometimes on what appeared to be a collision course. However, both girls managed somehow to avoid hitting each other, nimbly maneuvering in front or to the side. Then, it was over. The two dancers froze, toes pointed again, and made their bows.

"You looked fantastic, honey!" said Mr. Hubbard as Caitlin returned to the camp.

"I thought you were the best!" added Kaylee.

Mrs. Hubbard hugged her daughter, then nervously examined her to make sure she hadn't ruined anything in the process.

Caitlin danced again a short time later. After that, she had a long break before her third dance. “Thank goodness!” cried Caitlin melodramatically. “Where’s my bagel?”

Mrs. Hubbard eyed her daughter nervously. “Your next dance is on stage five,” said Mrs. Hubbard. “I’ll need to go to that room and see if they’re moving through the dance groups faster than on stage seven. Maybe you should wait.”

Caitlin rolled her eyes and let her jaw sag as if she were on the verge of death. “Mom, I’m going to pass out from malnutrition!”

Finally Mrs. Hubbard conceded and had Caitlin slip on a navy blue smock to protect her dress from stains and crumbs.

Kaylee could have sworn that Caitlin finished her bagel in three bites.

Afterwards, Caitlin asked her parents if she could explore the feis. “I’ve never been to one before, and so far, all I’ve seen is the inside of this one room!”

Caitlin’s mother examined her watch nervously.

“Be back in twenty minutes,” said her father. Caitlin squealed in delight and the two girls scurried off.

It was still an hour before noon, but Kaylee noticed that everything seemed busier than when she and Mr. Hubbard had ventured out earlier. In addition to the vendors she had noticed previously, Kaylee now spied a photographer who would take your picture in your dance dress, a dance shoe dealer and a vendor selling Irish music CDs and DVDs.

Caitlin’s eyes were wide. “This place has everything!”

Suddenly, a familiar voice cut through the buzz of the crowd. “Hey, O’Shrimp, did you forget you were supposed to wear a dress?”

It was Brittany Hall. She wore shimmering gold jam pants, a white top and her curly blonde dance wig. A gold medal attached to a green and white ribbon hung around her neck.

Kaylee's voice could hardly have expressed less enthusiasm. "Hi Brittany." She noticed the expression of muted horror on Caitlin's face as it dawned on her that this was the girl who constantly picked on her best friend. "I'm just here watching Caitlin today."

At this, Caitlin mustered a tight-lipped smile, but Kaylee could tell that it took almost all of her friend's bagel-fueled energy.

"Oh well," said Brittany casually, "you'll be ready someday."

"I'm ready now," Kaylee said quickly. "I'll be dancing at the Snowfeis in Milwaukee."

"I did twenty-one feisanna last year," said Brittany. She lifted the ribbon a couple of inches, bringing her medal to chin level. "Got this in my slip jig today!" Then Brittany turned to Caitlin. "How'd you do today?"

Caitlin said that she hadn't checked the results.

"Are you in Beginner?" Brittany asked, sizing up Caitlin. "I'm in Open." She said this the way someone might say, "I ended world hunger," or "I'm the Queen of England".

"Beginner Two," said Caitlin, her eyes narrowing to angry slits. "I've only been dancing a little over a year. Kaylee and I will probably be in Open by next year!"

Brittany laughed as if she were talking to the class dunces. "That's not how it works. You usually spend at least a whole year at the same level. Then you move up in January of the next year—if you get high enough scores! Some dancers spend years at the same level!" As she said this, she cast a weary glance at Kaylee.

Kaylee wanted to pull Brittany's wig down over her eyes and kick her in the shins, but she was too interested in what her rival had said. "So how long will it take us to get to the Open level?"

Brittany shook her head. "Don't they teach you anything at your dance school? If you get top scores in all your Beginner Two dances this year, you'll be in Novice next year. You have to get top scores in all your Novice dances to move up into Open!"

Kaylee's face fell. It would be at least two years before she would be as good as Brittany.

"Of course," Brittany continued, addressing Caitlin, "by the time you get into Open, I'll have gone through Pre-champion to the Champion level!"

Then she turned to Kaylee. "And by the time *you* get into Open, O'Shrimp, I'll be a grandmother!" She laughed at her own joke, whirled around, the lights flashing splendidly off her sequined jams, and then sauntered off.

Caitlin glowered after her and then gave her friend a hug. "I told you those Golden Academy girls are jerks!"

"I always thought it would be cool to practice really hard and someday beat Brittany in competition," said Kaylee sullenly. "I guess that's never going to happen."

"You've already beaten her where it's important," said Caitlin.

"What do you mean?" asked Kaylee.

Caitlin offered a big smile. "You're a much nicer person than she is." This made Kaylee smile, too, and then the two girls began to run toward the food vendors as they realized that their time was almost up—and Mrs. Hubbard would not be happy.

Fourteen

The Sunday morning after the Winter Arts Feis, Kaylee was up early, energized by what she had seen the previous day—and by what was going to happen today.

The excitement of being at her first feis had made her wish the weeks would fly past until the Milwaukee Snowfeis. She wanted to be out there on stage in her school dress, smiling, her arms straight, her toes pointed. She wanted to be part of the rainbow of costumes and music and voices.

It had been fun to watch Caitlin dance and to see the thrill on her friend's face when she went to the results posters at the end of the day and saw that she had earned two fifth-place ribbons.

"I'll carry these with me until I die!" Caitlin had said, her smile so big Kaylee wondered whether her face might crack. "I can't believe I got ribbons at my very first feis!"

However, Kaylee's energy was also amped up because today she would be playing with her old soccer team, the Green Storm.

Caitlin had frowned when Kaylee mentioned it again on their way back from Chicago, warning her of all the potential dangers—the greatest of which was Miss Helen.

"How could Miss Helen ever find out?" Kaylee had asked. "She hates soccer. She's not going to show up at the Paavo Sports Complex to cheer on one of the teams and see me out there."

Caitlin had conceded the point. "Just be careful."

After breakfast and church, Mrs. O'Shay headed off to the Stitchin' Kitchen, but she returned about twenty minutes later. "Grandma's going to watch the store for awhile so I can see your game," she explained. "I hardly ever got to see you play the past two years. This will be fun!"

"Will Grandma be okay by herself?" asked Kaylee.

"She'll be fine for a couple of hours," said Mrs. O'Shay. "Besides, Will is there, too. He'll look out for her."

Kaylee seemed surprised. "Will?"

Tom O'Shay came into the kitchen at this point. "We gave him a choice between going to see your soccer game or spending the afternoon watching your grandmother. He chose Grandma."

Kaylee listened to soccer advice from her father the entire ten mile drive to the Paavo Sports Complex, a huge building with three indoor soccer pitches. When they entered the building, Kaylee saw the green jerseys of her teammates near the middle field and started to jog in that direction until she was interrupted by a shout. She turned to her left. To her surprise, Caitlin stood waving with Mrs. Hubbard. Kaylee slowed and trotted over to where they stood.

"We only live half a mile away," explained Caitlin. "I thought I'd come and stand watch."

Kaylee was confused. "Stand watch?"

Caitlin smiled. "Yeah. If I see Miss Helen come through the door, I'll let out a yell and you can hide before she sees you."

Both girls laughed.

"About time you got here!"

Kaylee turned in the direction of this familiar voice. Jackie stood a few feet away, looking irritated.

Kaylee moved to give Jackie a hug, but Jackie took a half-step backward. "Come on! We've got to warm up!"

Half-turning toward Caitlin, she spoke to Jackie over a shoulder. "This is my friend Caitlin. She lives here in Paavo."

Jackie's gaze could not have been much cooler. "I suppose she's one of those *dancer* girls." She pronounced the word "dancer" as if it were something she had discovered under a rock. Caitlin stopped smiling.

"Let's get going!" insisted Jackie. "We're not going to beat the Yellow Clash by dancing!"

Kaylee waved goodbye to Caitlin and followed Jackie through the opening at their box and onto the pitch.

"What's up with you?" asked Kaylee as they jogged toward the sea of green jerseys passing balls in front of one of the goals. "You're so crabby today!"

"I just think you should be concentrating on the game," said Jackie sternly, "not bringing your dancer friends to distract you. This isn't some big slumber party, you know!"

It took a moment for Kaylee to realize how far her mouth had dropped open. "She came here on her own! She lives in Paavo!"

"Whatever!" said Jackie, turning her back on Kaylee and kicking a ball away from the equipment bag.

While the rest of the girls on the Green Storm chattered excitedly during warm-up drills, Kaylee and Jackie remained silent. Kaylee felt confused and hurt, unable to understand why Jackie was being so mean. Then the teams lined up for the start, and Kaylee joined her father and Mr. Kizobu in the box at the side of the field.

The field looked a lot like a big hockey rink with plexi-glass walls and two long boxes on one side where each team had a bench. Unlike a hockey rink, the playing surface here was dark-green artificial grass. The Green Storm bench stood empty except for a row of water bottles and Kaylee. The Green Storm was short on players, but had enough for a full team plus one substitute. Mr. Kizobu had decided that Kaylee would sit the bench first, since she was not a regular member of the team. As the referee placed the game ball at the center of the field, Kaylee looked across and noticed Caitlin smiling and waving from a small row of aluminum bleacher seats on the far side. *At least* she *still likes me*, thought Kaylee.

The game began, and right away, the twin Valentine sisters on the Yellow Clash took control. Chrissy Valentine, quick and an excellent ball handler, scored a goal just two minutes into the first half. Debbie Valentine scored a few minutes later, and Kaylee began to wonder whether the Green Storm would stand much of a chance. Then, just moments after the ball was put back into play, Brittany Hall scored for the Green Storm. She scored a second goal on a free kick after being tripped up by Debbie Valentine.

I hate to admit it, but Brittany really is good, thought Kaylee.

Suddenly, Kaylee heard her own name being called, and she hustled onto the field to replace Kari Sorgi at the midfielder position.

It felt good to be in a soccer game again. Kaylee hustled and played strong defense. Most of her passes went where she wanted. Best of all, she did not do anything to embarrass herself in front of her Green Storm teammates or Caitlin. At halftime, after another goal by Chrissy Valentine and a counterstrike by Heather Chandler, the score remained tied at three.

As the girls sucked down water near the sideline, Mr. Kizobu tried to keep the message positive. "The Yellow Clash is good, but you girls are hanging right with them! I just hope they don't wear us down in the second half!"

Early in the second half, with Kaylee back on the bench, Chrissy Valentine scored her third goal of the game to give the Clash the lead. "Still plenty of time," Kaylee's father yelled as the girls lined up for the kick-off. A few minutes later, Kaylee was ordered into the game to give Heather a break at forward.

"You always find a way to mess it up, O'Shrimp," warned Brittany as Kaylee jogged near her. "Just get the ball to me, and I'll do the rest!"

For awhile, the Valentine sisters kept the ball near the Green Storm goal, but then Jackie sent a kick down the sideline where Kaylee controlled it. As she brought the ball up, she spotted Brittany near the goal, her hand waving frantically. "I'm open!"

But she wasn't. Two Clash defenders stood on either side of her. Instead of passing, Kaylee continued up the sidelines and then tried to get it to Maddie Evans. However, her pass was stolen by a Clash defender.

The ball headed back toward the Green Storm side of the field, but once again, Jackie came up with it, sending the ball into Clash territory. Maddie controlled it in the middle but suddenly found herself trapped by two Clash players. The three of them struggled for the ball, and suddenly it popped out toward Kaylee.

As Kaylee stopped the ball, she once again heard Brittany's voice. "Open!" And once again, Kaylee noticed that Brittany was tightly covered by two Clash defenders. She decided to keep the ball herself and bring it up the sidelines, since no one seemed near. She made the turn and began her dribble, but then she caught sight of someone out of the corner of her eye. Brittany had broken away from the defenders and was now only a few feet from Kaylee.

"Give me the ball, O'Shrimp!"

Surprised and even a little intimidated, Kaylee tapped a pass to her. However, the two defenders closed quickly, and the ball squirted away, back to Kaylee. She decided to try to take it around them. The defenders let Brittany go and began to chase Kaylee.

Brittany's in the open! thought Kaylee. *All she has to do is cut toward the goal and I'll pass it to her. It'll be an easy score!*

Incredibly, instead of doing what was clearly the most logical thing for her to have done, Brittany chased after Kaylee and the two defenders.

No! thought Kaylee.

"Give me that ball, you loser!" grunted Brittany as she lowered her shoulder between the two Clash players. She knocked them off balance as she sliced through the group, stealing the ball away from Kaylee. As the first Clash player stumbled, trying to keep from falling, her feet tangled with Kaylee's and both went down hard onto the pitch. The second Clash player tumbled onto the top of them. Kaylee heard a snap and felt a sudden intense pain in her right leg. The referee's whistle stopped play and everyone sat down. Kaylee heard crying, and after an instant, she realized it was coming from *her*!

"Kaylee!" cried her father, who had rushed out from the box and now knelt over her. "Where does it hurt?"

Kaylee pointed to her leg.

Now she saw Mr. Kizobu beside her father. He appeared to be looking at her leg, his head shaking back and forth.

"I'm no doctor, Tom," he said to Kaylee's father. "But that looks like it's broken to me!"

Fifteen

Dr. Holland let her see the x-ray.

"It's a break all right." He pointed to the clear line just above the ankle in a bone he referred to as the "distal tibia". This news had caused Kaylee to cry. She had spent a lot of time crying since the fall, and a part of her wondered how she could still have any tears left.

When she had gone to the emergency room on Saturday, the young doctor there had wrapped the leg in what he called a "soft cast" and had advised her to see her family doctor or an orthopedist in a few days. "Once the swelling goes down."

Now Dr. Holland would apply a hard cast. "One that all of your friends can sign."

This made Kaylee cry even more. Friends? What friends did she have now? Jackie was mad at her because Caitlin had come to the soccer match. Caitlin was mad at her because she had warned Kaylee not to play soccer, Kaylee had ignored the warning and had gotten hurt. The referee had tossed Brittany out of the game after the fateful play that had injured Kaylee and shaken up two Clash players. With Kaylee and Brittany gone, the Storm was a player short on the field. As a result, the Clash easily won the game as they wore down their opponents, who had no substitutes to call off the bench. Kaylee's Green Storm teammates blamed her for this. "If she hadn't been such a ball hog and had just passed it to Brittany, none of this would have ever happened!" Heather had said rather too loudly as the emergency medical technicians loaded Kaylee onto the stretcher.

She had cost the team the game and had lost her two best friends. These were awful things, but the worst was still to come: Now there was no way to keep Miss Helen from finding that Kaylee had played soccer. She could hardly bear to think about what her teacher would say to her.

As badly as Kaylee felt, she knew that her father felt worse. "I talked you into this," he said over and over. "I'm the one who's to blame. I'm so sorry, honey."

"I wanted to play," Kaylee had said. "If anyone is to blame, it's—"

She was going to say Brittany's name, but her father finished the sentence for her. "Those darned Yellow Clash defenders who got you all tangled up!"

Kaylee sighed. Somehow her father never seemed to notice Brittany's dark side.

"The cast will have to stay on for four to six weeks," said Dr. Holland as he applied the hard cast on Wednesday.

Kaylee almost started crying again. "But I'm supposed to have a dance competition four weeks from this Saturday!"

Dr. Holland scratched his chin. "Well, everyone heals differently. Maybe you're a fast healer. But even if the cast were to come off after only four weeks, the muscles in that leg would still be pretty weak compared to the other one." He turned to Kaylee's mother. "This dance competition . . . is it a once-in-a-lifetime opportunity like walking on the moon or meeting the President?"

Beth O'Shay looked into her daughter's pleading eyes, and it hurt to answer. "Not really. There are dance competitions throughout the year. I've already got her signed up for a Feis in Madison in June."

Dr. Holland nodded as if he had suspected as much. "Better to err on the side of caution. Remove your cast too early and you could have problems."

Kaylee persisted. "But the cast *might* come off in four weeks, right? June is almost forever!"

Now a slight smile tickled the corners of Dr. Holland's mouth. "We'll x-ray it again in four weeks. If your break has healed properly, I'll power up the cast saw."

Now Kaylee's green eyes burned with a fierce hope. She saw herself dancing at the Snowfeis as stuck-up girls from other schools looked on, amazed to see such an incredible performance from someone who got out of a cast only three days ago. Then the daydream ended and she was back in Dr. Holland's office, being helped toward the door by her mother.

Dr. Holland called after them, "If you want those bones to be strong and heal quickly, I'd advise you to drink a lot of milk, young lady!"

Kaylee drank five glasses before bed that night.

"There'll be nothing left for my cereal tomorrow morning!" Will complained.

In school on Thursday, Kaylee got plenty of sympathy—from her teachers. Jackie hardly spoke to her, however, and Brittany and Heather simply snickered whenever they saw her hobble past on her crutches in the hallway.

She drank three cartons of milk during lunch. Her teacher became concerned after writing Kaylee's fourth restroom pass.

After school, her mother spoke to her about dance. "It's too bad you'll have to miss dance for the next four weeks." Then she frowned. "And it's too bad those lessons were all paid for in advance."

Kaylee spoke up abruptly. "Take me to dance class tonight."

Her mother looked surprised. “Why? You can’t dance, Kaylee.”

Kaylee looked at the floor. “I should tell my teachers what happened. I feel like I let them down.”

Mrs. O’Shay’s eyes darkened. “It’s that awful Miss Helen, isn’t it? She’s the one who’s got you thinking like that.”

Kaylee said nothing.

“You don’t owe her any explanation,” said Mrs. O’Shay with anger that surprised Kaylee. “If you want to dance and play soccer too, that’s your business! Accidents happen. You didn’t plan this!”

“I still want to go,” pleaded Kaylee. “You said the classes were paid for. I can learn by watching.”

Mrs. O’Shay thought for a moment and then shrugged. “I guess it’s fine with me.”

They drove to Paavo. Some parents sat in chairs in the carpeted area near the front door and chatted during dance classes. Others drove off to run errands. When Kaylee’s mother brought her to dance class, she usually sat in her car reading a book. On this evening, however, she accompanied her daughter to the door.

Annie Delaney saw Kaylee first, and her green eyes went wide in surprise behind her oval glasses. “Oh no!” she said, her voice full of sadness. “What happened?”

Kaylee told the story, holding back a tear or two in a couple of spots.

Annie knelt down and gave Kaylee a hug. “You poor dear! And with your first feis coming up next month!”

Kaylee wiped her eyes. “Dr. Holland says some people are quick healers.”

Annie smiled, but it seemed the sort of smile people offer up when they are trying to mask their true feelings. “I’ll bet you’re one of the quick ones!” Then

Annie stood and faced Mrs. O'Shay. "I'm so sorry. I suppose we won't be seeing Kaylee for awhile."

"Actually," said Kaylee's mother, "she wants to come and watch if that's okay."

"By all means!" said Annie, breaking into the warm smile that was more common.

Mrs. O'Shay thanked Annie and headed back to her car and book. Kaylee hobbled to the edge of the carpeted area and found a chair. April, Meghan and a few of the other girls rushed over to give her hugs and hear what had happened, as did her teacher, Tara. Caitlin hung at the back of the group.

Eventually Tara and the girls headed out onto the dance floor to begin their stretching exercises. However, after a few minutes, Kaylee felt a sensation like she was not alone. She turned to her left and saw Miss Helen in her usual plain, dark sweats standing above her like a medieval fortress.

"What is this?" Miss Helen pointed to the cast.

Kaylee felt an icy fear inside and found herself on the verge of tears again. Instead, she gritted her teeth and spoke very softly. "I broke my leg."

Miss Helen's eyes were frigid, blue daggers. "How?" Kaylee was certain she had already guessed the answer. Again she gritted her teeth.

"In an indoor soccer game on Sunday."

Miss Helen stood up straight, the daggers in her eyes a lethal cobalt. The muscles in her jaw seemed to bulge as if they were straining against an enormous impulse to speak. Then, with a great sigh, she turned and walked out onto the dance floor.

Never had Kaylee wanted to cry so badly. Her body shook slightly with the effort it took to hold back the flood. *She thinks I'm just like Lizzie Martin,* thought Kaylee. *She thinks soccer is more important to me than dance.*

Maybe Miss Helen was right. A week ago, Caitlin and Jackie had been her best friends and she had been ready to dance in her first feis. Now, it looked as if she had thrown everything away.

She looked at the cast on her leg. Dr. Holland had asked her what color she wanted. There had never been any question in her mind: navy-blue, just like her Trean Gaoth school dress.

Kaylee looked out at her friends and the two teachers on the dance floor.

I'll show her that she's wrong!

Sixteen

The following Thursday, it snowed four inches. The wind blew a stinging, horizontal spray of ice crystals that made it difficult to see fifty meters. About half of the girls in Kaylee's dance class lived right in Paavo, so even in nasty weather, a session was rarely cancelled.

Twenty-five girls normally attended Kaylee's Thursday night class. Because of the horrid weather, this evening's class consisted of Caitlin, April, Meghan and six other girls. Miss Helen shook the ice off her shabby, massive coat that smelled of cigarettes and draped it over a wire hanger near the door. She removed her boots, large and black and perfect for a trek to the Arctic Circle. She slipped on large, worn ghillies and approached the small group on the wide, wooden floor.

"I am afraid that you are stuck with me tonight," she said matter-of-factly to her students. "Tara will not be here. Her car is stuck in a snow bank."

The girls began chattering about the dangers each of them had faced in getting to Trean Gaoth Academy that evening.

"All right," Miss Helen said finally. "You have all shown much dedication by being here tonight. Now let's start our stretching. You won't become great dancers by telling stories."

A minute later, the glass front door swung open again, letting in a swirl of ice crystals and a blast of cold.

"Another brave soul!" remarked Miss Helen, turning with the others to see who had just arrived. She was surprised to see that this one tottered on crutches. Her mother helped her remove her coat, hung it, and then retreated out the door.

Kaylee hobbled across the carpet to the edge of the dance floor. Then she rested the crutches against a chair and sat down on the carpeted floor. Miss Helen noticed that she was dressed in dance shorts and a Trean Gaoth t-shirt.

"You came through that weather to watch us dance?" asked Miss Helen incredulously.

"All the way from Rosemary," said Kaylee quietly. "But I didn't come to just watch."

With that, Kaylee began doing stretching exercises.

Miss Helen watched for a moment, a quizzical look on her face. Then she turned back to the others. "All right, girls. Let's get started."

Seventeen

The aptly-named Snowfeis drew closer. In fact, it seemed to snow almost every other day in Rosemary and Paavo.

"Business has actually been pretty good at the Stitchin' Kitchen," Kaylee's mother reported.

Her father laughed. "That's probably because everybody's making quilts to keep warm!"

Despite the nasty weather, Kaylee did not miss a practice at Trean Gaoth. Mr. Kizobu had done some research online and come up with a list of exercises she could do in order to keep herself reasonably fit despite her cast. She did these—as well as sit-ups and her regular dance stretching—while her Trean Gaoth friends danced their normal routines. She also watched them carefully, taking notes on a little pad with a purple kitten on the cover, notes on anything that she thought she should remember in order to make herself a better dancer. When she had completed all of her stretching and exercises two or three times, she would walk back and forth from one end of the building to the other—using her crutches of course—until her arms ached. Then she would stand, supporting herself with the crutches, at the edge of the dance floor, and try to imitate the dance steps without putting weight on her injured leg.

Doing these things, Kaylee kept herself in motion for most of the hour and a half at Trean Gaoth Academy. By the time Caitlin and the others finished, she often felt just as tired as if she had been on the dance floor with them.

Annie and Tara often mentioned how proud they were of her hard work. She sometimes caught Miss Helen staring at her with that quizzical look she had given Kaylee the day of the big snow storm, but the older teacher usually said nothing.

You think I'm like Lizzie Martin, thought Kaylee. *But I'm not anything like her!*

For the first two weeks after she had been injured, Caitlin seemed to ignore Kaylee at dance practice. This hurt Kaylee far more than the broken leg. Then, on the third Thursday, Caitlin stopped next to Kaylee, who was already sitting on the floor, stretching. Caitlin opened her bag and pulled out a pair of gloves, which she dropped on the floor in front of Kaylee.

"Here. I thought you could use this."

Kaylee picked up the black and red gloves, which appeared to be leather. "Thanks, I guess."

"They're my old batting gloves from when I used to play in a summer softball league," explained Caitlin. "I heard you tell April that you were getting blisters from the crutches and I thought they might help."

Kaylee looked down at the gloves and then back up at Caitlin. Suddenly, both girls smiled.

"Thanks," said Kaylee, and her problems seemed to fly away, carried off on a strong wind.

Caitlin hurried onto the dance floor and Kaylee slipped on the gloves. As she tried them with the crutches, she noticed an immediate improvement. When Caitlin looked over, Kaylee gave her an enthusiastic thumbs-up—almost losing her balance in the process.

At the end of practice, Annie came up to her after Caitlin had gone. "You're awfully dedicated, Kaylee," said Annie, kneeling next to her as Kaylee pulled on the loose-fitting sweat pants that would protect her legs and cast from the snow.

"The Snowfeis is two weeks from this Saturday," said Kaylee. "I'm hoping the doctor will cut off my cast in time!"

Annie shook her head. "I've never seen an eleven-year-old work so hard!"

"I think it's because my dad's a soccer coach," said Kaylee, but then she looked around guiltily to see whether Miss Helen was standing nearby. Seeing no sign of her, Kaylee continued. "He'd always take me out to the park and we'd practice dribbling or kicking goals. Sometimes we'd do it for a couple of hours. If he couldn't go with me, I'd sometimes do it on my own."

Annie nodded very slightly. "There's more to it than that, though. Sometimes a person's passion is powered by love. I see that in you. You absolutely love Irish dance. So do I! That's a good thing."

Kaylee nodded and smiled.

"But I also see something else driving you. I can see it in your eyes like a little green storm."

Kaylee did not say anything, but she thought of how badly she wanted to dance at the Snowfeis in order to show Brittany and Miss Helen that they were wrong.

"Nothing wrong with a bit of a stormy personality," said Annie kindly. "After all, you and I, we're both Irish!"

This brought the smile back to Kaylee's face.

"Just make sure the love is always more powerful than the storm," said Annie, who then rose to her feet and walked over to where Tara was speaking with a parent.

Kaylee was not quite sure what Annie meant, but she certainly agreed with one thing: She loved Irish dance.

Eighteen

Kaylee could remember being this excited a few times before.

Christmas. Big soccer games. Her first day at Trean Gaoth Academy.

But never at the doctor's office.

Her mother sat with her, nervously tapping her fingers on the arm of the padded plastic chair in Dr. Holland's examination room.

"Everything looks fine here," Dr. Holland said during a quick visual examination of her leg. "Everything except . . ."

"Except what?" asked Kaylee breathlessly.

"Except I can hardly see the cast!"

Kaylee sighed with relief and both Dr. Holland and Mrs. O'Shay chuckled. After Caitlin had gotten over her disappointment with her friend's injury, she had taken a metallic glitter marker and written a message that almost completely covered the cast.

"We'll get a quick x-ray to make sure everything is coming along just the way we want it." Then he turned to Kaylee and gave her a serious look. "You've been drinking plenty of milk, I hope?"

Mrs. O'Shay laughed humorlessly. "We need to buy our own cow!"

A nurse escorted Kaylee to the x-ray room, and in a few minutes, she was back sitting with her mother.

"Relax," said Beth O'Shay, noticing her daughter chewing her fingernails, which she normally never did. "It's going to be fine."

Kaylee smiled, but what she really felt were the gremlins doing somersaults in her stomach.

It seemed like forever before Dr. Holland finally returned. He held a folder from which he pulled two x-rays and clipped them onto a lighted viewing screen on one wall of the examination room. He studied them carefully for almost a minute and then invited Kaylee and her mother to come close.

"The bones are knitting together very nicely," said Dr. Holland brightly. "I think two more weeks and you can say goodbye to this cast forever."

Kaylee's face bypassed "shocked" and "disappointed" and roared all the way to "panicked". "Two more weeks? You mean it's not coming off today?"

Dr. Holland seemed mildly surprised. "When I put the cast on you, Kaylee, I told you that it would be four to six weeks."

Kaylee could hardly choke out the words. "But you said it might come off in four!"

Dr. Holland's face sagged sadly, but then he gathered himself and pointed to the back-lighted x-rays. "As I said before, Kaylee, everyone heals a little differently. And this x-ray shows that you definitely are healing. You just don't have quite enough callous formed."

"But I need the cast off now!" she cried. "The Snowfeis is this Saturday!"

"That might not be the best idea," said Dr. Holland patiently. "If you try to do too much too soon, you might end up in a cast for several additional weeks. You could even knock the bones out of place and we'd have to put you under anesthesia to realign them."

Mrs. O'Shay gathered her daughter in a hug. "Oh, honey, don't be sad. The feis in Madison will be here before you know it."

Kaylee was surprised that she did not feel the urge to cry. What she felt was anger.

Anger at Dr. Holland for not cutting off the cast.

Anger at her mother for not forcing Dr. Holland to cut off the cast.

Anger at her stupid slow-growing bones.

Anger at Brittany Hall for crashing into her and causing the injury.

But mostly she felt anger at herself—and she was not quite sure why. *I didn't cause this*, she told herself.

Or did I?

When she got home, Kaylee grabbed the telephone, closed herself into her room and phoned Caitlin.

"Oh no!" cried her friend. "Oh, Kaylee! I know how much you were looking forward to this feis!"

Kaylee waited a long time before responding. In her mind, she could see Brittany laughing. *You always find a way to mess it up, O'Shrimp!* She saw Miss Helen shaking her head in an I-told-you-so way.

"I'm still looking forward to it," Kaylee finally said.

"What do you mean?" asked Caitlin.

"I'm going to Snowfeis!" said Kaylee resolutely. "And I'm going to dance!"

Nineteen

Kaylee had imagined riding to the Milwaukee Snowfeis with her parents, full of excitement, hoping to do well. She had imagined her mother fussing to make sure she looked just right. She had imagined her father proudly watching her first dances.

Instead, she rode to the feis with the Hubbards. The cast still held her foot prisoner and her crutches were tucked beside her. Kaylee's parents had elected not to come, since Kaylee would not be dancing. However, they had not minded that she rode with the Hubbards to watch Caitlin.

What her parents did not know—what no one, in fact, knew except for Caitlin—was that Kaylee would be dancing at the Snowfeis after all. "I can't believe I'm helping you with your evil plan," Caitlin had told her.

Kaylee had patted her on the shoulder. "If your best friend won't help you with an evil plan, who will?"

Kaylee's evil plan had three problems to overcome. First, she had to find a way to get her registration materials. Second, she had to remove the cast. Third, she had to get dressed without the Hubbard parents knowing.

Caitlin identified a fourth potential problem. "What if you dance and your foot breaks again because it's not completely healed? It could be months before you get another chance! Maybe you'll break it worse and they'll have to amputate your leg!"

"It's not going to break," said Kaylee. "Relax." Then a shiver ran down her spine as she realized how similar this sounded to the reassurances she had given Caitlin before she had played in the tragic soccer game.

The Milwaukee Snowfeis was being held at the Golden Academy of Irish Dance near the Cream City Mall. Because Kaylee still hobbled along on crutches, Mr. Hubbard dropped them all off at the front door and then went across the street to park his car in the mall lot. *I guess he'll be pretty surprised at the end of the day when I walk out like a normal person,* thought Kaylee. Somehow this thought did not make her feel as happy as she had expected.

They joined dozens of other dancers and parents moving through the stylish glass and steel main entrance. Above the brilliantly-windowed main foyer, which was large enough for almost any respectable hotel, a metallic gold sign greeted them with the words, *Simply the Best!*

"They'll probably serve caviar at the snack booth!" said Caitlin, and Kaylee could hear the stiffness in her voice.

Tables had been set up in the foyer for registration, and it took only a moment for Mrs. Hubbard to collect her daughter's materials. Then they moved ahead into the *Bernard Golden Hall,* named after the academy director's father. Six stages had been set up in this room, which was the size of a gymnasium.

"There are three other dance stages set up in other rooms, but all of your dances are here," noted Mrs. Hubbard as Caitlin peeked over her elbow at the schedule.

They spread a blanket, set up a couple of folding chairs and then Caitlin's mother began to get nervous about everything just as she had at the Winter Arts Feis.

"What a place!" said Mr. Hubbard as he returned from parking the car. "It's like a fancy health club!"

Caitlin sniffed. "I prefer bowling alleys. At least our school doesn't make it look like we're showing off."

Mr. Hubbard nodded, not necessarily in agreement, Kaylee observed, but probably to avoid an argument. Then he raised an eyebrow toward Kaylee. "Bagel?"

Kaylee shook her head. "I think I'll wait." In truth, she was starving, but she was too nervous to eat. Besides, she and Caitlin had an evil plan to put into motion. Mr. Hubbard shrugged and disappeared in the direction of the vendors.

"Let's start by gluing your socks," Mrs. Hubbard said to her daughter.

"Can I use the bathroom first?" asked Caitlin. Her mother nodded, the nervous energy radiating from her eyes growing to a near-lethal level.

"Don't waste time," she told Caitlin and Kaylee as they headed off. "Dancing starts at 8:30!"

"That probably means about 9:15," whispered Caitlin as the girls disappeared out the door.

They stopped near the registration tables. "Are you sure?" asked Caitlin, her eyes pleading: *No. You're my friend. Don't do this.*

Kaylee was adamant. "I'm not going to miss this feis!" Caitlin sighed and shuffled off to the restroom. Kaylee stepped to one of the tables and addressed a middle-aged man in thick eyeglasses. "Can I pick up my registration things?"

The man looked over the top of his glasses at her crutches. "You don't look like you're ready to dance today, young lady."

"This happened after we signed up," explained Kaylee, pointing to her leg. "I still want my number and stuff for my scrapbook at home."

The man smiled benevolently and dug through a long file box, pulling out number 924. He handed this to

Kaylee along with a length of white ribbon, a feis booklet and a stage schedule.

As Kaylee hobbled away awkwardly, attempting to hold onto her goodies while operating the crutches, the man said, "Hope you get that cast off soon, dear."

Me too, thought Kaylee. *Like in about ten minutes!*

Caitlin returned, glanced disapprovingly at the materials tucked between Kaylee's arm and crutch, and the two headed back to their camp.

Mr. Hubbard was still off getting breakfast. A folding stool had been set up on which Caitlin plopped herself, waiting for the glue. Mrs. Hubbard opened a small backpack and pulled out the clear bottle, her back to Kaylee.

This was Kaylee's chance. She unzipped her friend's dress bag. Underneath Caitlin's school dress they had smuggled Kaylee's. She carefully slipped it out along with a plastic shopping sack, and then re-zipped the bag.

Every time she looked at the navy and gold dress with the Trean Gaoth logo, the beauty of it took her breath away. The fact that her grandmother had spent almost a hundred hours sewing it overwhelmed her. Kaylee tied the shopping bag to a belt loop, grabbed the hook of the hanger holding the dress, held her number in her teeth and tottered away. Mrs. Hubbard, completely absorbed in preparing her daughter for battle, noticed nothing.

Kaylee had imagined that her biggest problem after smuggling away her dress would be making sure she did not run into Mr. Hubbard until after her cast was off and there was nothing anyone could do to stop her. However, with the bag hanging awkwardly from one side, her competitor number in her mouth, and her dress hooked precariously over the top of a crutch, Kaylee found it almost impossible to move. She made awkward, jerking motions that took her a few feet, and then had to stop to steady the dress or readjust the position of the bag. Her goal was to make it across the room to stage three. That was where her first dance, the reel, would be contested. As luck would have it, a restroom door opened only a short distance from that stage. In one of those restroom stalls, Kaylee would cut off her hated cast.

She had barely covered a quarter of the distance when she lost her balance and let out a gasp, catching herself at the last moment with a crutch placed at an extremely odd angle. Her competitor number flew out of her mouth and landed on the floor about ten feet in front of her. *Great! How am I going to pick that up? There's no place to hang my dress, nothing to lean my crutches against, and both of my hands are full!*

As she leaned at an absurd angle, frozen like a work of abstract dance art, Kaylee heard a voice behind her.

"Do you need help?"

Kaylee turned her head—which was about the only thing she could move without upsetting her delicate balance and crashing to the floor—and saw two girls about her age in dance wigs and dark green smocks that protected their costumes when they were not on stage.

"Sure," said Kaylee, and immediately the two girls carefully began to nudge her into an upright position. The taller of the two bent down and picked up Kaylee's number. The other took her dress and the shopping bag.

The short girl burst into a great smile. "My name's Jordi. It looked like you were in real trouble, so I said to Hannah, *Let's help her before she breaks something else!*"

Hannah looked at Kaylee's number, clearly puzzled. "Are you going to dance today?"

"Can you do that?" asked Jordi, astonished. "In a cast?"

At first, Kaylee was reluctant to say anything. But these girls did not seem to want to get her into trouble. They simply wanted to help.

"The doctor was supposed to cut my cast off last week," explained Kaylee, conveniently leaving out a great many pertinent facts. "He didn't. I don't want to miss my first feis."

"I remember my first feis last year," said Jordi, chatting as if they had been friends for a century. "I wouldn't have wanted to miss it, either."

"You're going to dance in a cast?" asked Hannah, her dark eyes as big as walnuts.

Kaylee revealed that the shopping bag contained a plastic covered dish holding her wig, pins, sock glue and a keyhole saw she had taken from her father's workbench.

"Wow!" said Jordi. "You really do want to dance!"

"I'm on stage three," said Kaylee, pointing.

"Us, too!" said Hannah. "We'll help you get there."

The going was much easier with Jordi and Hannah holding her gear. In just a few moments, they had reached the wall to the left of the stage and the two girls had settled her carefully onto a blanket. Jordi hung Kaylee's dress on a nearby rack filled with other dresses.

"That's my parents over there," said Jordi, pointing to a nicely-dressed man and woman standing beside chairs near stage three. The two just happened to look back toward the camp area at this moment, saw their daughter, smiled and waved.

"Hannah's parents are sitting somewhere over there, too, but I can't see them right now. Are your parents here?"

"Are you kidding?" asked Kaylee. "They'd kill me if they knew what I was planning."

Jordi looked puzzled. "I'd think they'd be mad at your doctor for not taking your cast off in time for the feis!"

Kaylee smiled weakly, remembering that she had not told Jordi about the possibility that she could seriously wreck her leg.

At this point, a voice came over the public address system, welcoming everyone to the Milwaukee Snowfeis hosted by Golden Academy of Irish Dance. Jordi and Hannah helped Kaylee to her feet as the Irish, Canadian and finally the U.S. national anthems were played. Kaylee looked at a clock on the wall. 8:30. Mrs. Hubbard would be beaming.

"I always get so excited at the start of a feis!" said Jordi, giving Kaylee such a big hug that she almost knocked her off her crutches.

Hannah nodded and then spoke to Kaylee as she began to loosen her smock. "Can you hang out with us today? It'll be fun!"

Kaylee smiled broadly at her two new friends. "Maybe for awhile."

"Yeah!" said Jordi enthusiastically. "We can show you all around this place! It's really cool!"

"Did you come to this feis last year?" asked Kaylee. "Is that how you know it so well?"

Jordi grinned proudly. "This is our school!"

Now the smocks were off and Kaylee saw the white dress and black stockings of the Golden Academy costume.

"You guys are from Golden?" Kaylee asked incredulously.

Both nodded happily. Then Hannah asked, "What's your school?"

Kaylee hesitated, then pointed to her dress on the rack. "Trean Gaoth."

"It's a beautiful dress!" said Jordi. Then she and Hannah both administered quick hugs to Kaylee. "Wish us luck!" cried Jordi. "We've got to get ready!"

They hurried off to the check-in area. Kaylee knew she would have to hurry as well. She hoped it would not take too long to saw off the cast. Getting dressed and putting on her wig could be done quickly, and she knew that she could probably count on help from Hannah and Jordi. According to the schedule, she was in the ninth dance on stage three.

She hopped on one foot to where the shopping bag rested against the wall. Kaylee pulled out the keyhole saw. In a moment, she would slip into the restroom and find an empty stall.

Then, after a few minutes of work, she would be free.

Music filled the air. Kaylee looked toward stage three, but dancing had not yet started there. To her right, she noticed that the first dance had gotten underway on stage two. A line of dancers stood at attention. Two advanced to center stage and began. Their steps were precise and they moved as if on glass. There were school dresses of almost every color, but many also wore solo costumes.

Now the next two dancers moved to center as the first two neared the end of their performance. It did not surprise Kaylee that she recognized one of the dancers in the next group.

Brittany Hall.

She leaped into action, toes perfectly pointed, leaps that seemed to suspend her in air, everything in perfect harmony with the accordion music. *How can someone so horrible dance so beautifully?* Kaylee wondered. She glanced into the crowd and spotted Brittany's father in the first row, a proud smile beneath his thick moustache.

You were wrong about me, Brittany, Kaylee thought as she watched. *I'm not going to mess this up.* She tightened her grip on the saw. Miss Helen was wrong, too. After this, everyone would know how much dance meant to her. She could feel the storm inside of her, dark and powerful.

Mr. Hall's head bobbed in time to the music, his eyes shining.

Kaylee twisted her head to stage three. Jordi's mother smoothed her dress and her father gave her a tiny kiss on the cheek, the final preparations before her dance.

Now Kaylee's eyes traveled to her school dress, still hanging on the rack. "A beautiful dress," Jordi had said. A dress her grandmother had labored over in secrecy for weeks, a dress stitched together with the thread of unconditional love.

Kaylee wished her grandmother would be there to see her dance in that dress at her first feis. But that would not be possible, because Kaylee's plan required secrecy. If she wanted it to succeed, no adults could know.

She wished that her parents could be there to see it. There would never be another first feis.

Just make sure the love is always more powerful than the storm, Annie had said.

She looked at the saw in her hand. Was she cutting off her cast today because she loved dance? Or did it have more to do with Brittany and Miss Helen? Just how powerful was the green storm inside of her?

Brittany had now finished her dance. In a few minutes, she would walk off stage two with the other girls in her group. She might walk right past Kaylee. Brittany would probably look at Kaylee's cast, shake her head, offer a comment about what a loser she was, how she couldn't even heal properly.

She looked back in the opposite direction where her new friends were now seated in chairs next to stage three, their faces radiant with the wonder and joy that is a part of dance.

Kaylee replaced the saw in the shopping bag. Then she hobbled on crutches to stage three where she could watch Jordi and Hannah.

The Madison feis in June suddenly did not seem so far off.

About the Author

Rod Vick is the author of *Kaylee's Choice* and the other books in the Kaylee O'Shay series.

The 2000 State Teacher of the Year, Rod Vick lives in Mukwonago, Wisconsin with his wife, Marsha, and children Haley and Joshua. He runs marathons, enthusiastically supports his children's dance and soccer passions, and pitches a pretty mean horseshoe.

Kaylee O'Shay, Irish Dancer
Book Three: Fire and Metal

When Kaylee's father loses his job and informs the family that they are moving, it sends a shock wave through the O'Shay house. For Kaylee, it means that she will be forced to leave her friends at school and at Trean Gaoth Academy of Irish Dance—and join Golden Academy, where she will face almost certain humiliation at the hands of her gifted but obnoxious rival, Brittany Hall.

For more information about the Kaylee O'Shay series, visit the official online site at www.kayleeoshay.com.

Acknowledgements

Thanks to My Lovely Wife Marsha, whose patience and understanding are critical pieces of the puzzle that allow me to write the Kaylee O'Shay books

Thanks to my daughter, Haley Marie, whose own passion for Irish dance inspired me to write about it. As she did with *Kaylee's Choice*, my daughter read the first draft of *Green Storm* and helped to make sure I kept it real. Sweetheart, I am so proud of you!

Thanks to two outstanding medical professionals for their help in answering questions related to issues in this book.

First, thank you to Dr. David Ban, a gifted physician whose expertise in the medical field is only exceeded by his caring, friendly personality.

Second, thanks to Dr. Steve Merkow, who first treated my own daughter, Haley, when she was just days old, and whose experience in orthopedics and with young athletes helped me immeasurably in dealing with my injured Kaylee.

Thanks to Emily Jacobs and Grace Dooley, whose wise suggestions helped me to create a great cover for this book.

Thanks to the people at Instantpublishing.com for their guidance.

Thank you to my father for teaching me to tell a story; and to my mother for teaching me to listen to them.

Made in the USA
Middletown, DE
08 June 2015